Sweet Healing

Love Happens • Book Eight

SUSAN WARNER

Sweet Healing

One

"You've faced angry townspeople before. Facing one man will be child's play."

Clarissa Hastings continued down the sidewalk. She knew that everyone was watching her as she strode through town in her four-inch heels and form-fitting dress. Today's dress had a flower print of large amaryllises, and she had paired it together with her red shoes. Her clothes were her armor, and she made sure she was armed every day. She made it her business to be out and about. She didn't want anyone to feel sorry for her or look too closely at her life.

Yesterday her world had been shaken for a moment when the council was told that Adam and Hannah Cade had decided to have their wedding here in Sweet Blooms. It would be the talk of the town, and it would be a media extravaganza. The thought of the media being around Sweet Blooms gave her pause. Last night she gave it some thought and realized she was overreacting. Today she was the untouchable queen. Then she saw a figure leaning against a car. He had a cowboy hat on that obscured his face, but it wouldn't have mattered. She knew that pose, that hat, and that man.

"It's just one man," Clarissa reiterated, taking sure strides toward the figure. "He can't say anything that matters now. If he wanted to say anything, he would have said it five years ago."

As if he could hear her, he pushed away from the car and stood in the middle of the block.

"I've gotten through worse," Clarissa said, then she lengthened her stride and found herself standing in front of him.

"Good morning, Clarissa. We need to talk," he said. "You look good."

Clarissa let the deep tones roll over her and seep into her soul. That voice had comforted her when she was at her lowest. That voice had encouraged her to follow her dreams. That voice had also abandoned her when she needed him the most.

"Step aside, Bain," she said in the most distant voice she could find. "You couldn't find me five years ago, so I don't know why you think you need to find me now."

He didn't say a thing; he just stood there.

Clarissa looked at him and realized he had no intention of moving. That feeling of nervous excitement was coming back. She didn't know how he did it, but it was as if he had never left. As if they had never been separated.

"Are you going to move, Bain?"

"I think I moved the last time and look where it left us," he said.

"It's done, so whatever." She took a step to show him how little she cared. Then it all went south. Bain reached out a hand towards her. Clarissa saw the hand and jumped back. She was so concerned about avoiding him that she lost her balance.

"Clarrie."

Clarissa heard the nickname he had for her and the world reverted to slow motion while her anger spiked beyond reason. She whipped around to face him. He grabbed her arms to save her. Realizing she was falling, she threw her arms around his neck, and as gravity pulled them down, Bain twisted, so Clarissa was above him. Before long, she felt the impact of the ground as she lay atop Bain.

She pushed herself up and looked down at him. Time had been good to Bain; he still had a muscular chest, broad shoulders, and it led up to a perfect jaw, a firm mouth, a slightly crooked nose, and the dark eyes with long lashes. Growing up, people had said he was pretty. When he broke his nose playing football, the team said he was handsome. Looking at the overall picture of the man beneath her, she thought he had to be one of the most gorgeous men on the planet. When she realized those eyes were staring back at her, she cleared her throat.

"Are you okay?" she asked, pushing away from him. She brought her knees up so she'd be able to stand up. "I'm not worried about your head because it's been hit by more weight than me—"

He gave her a lopsided smile. "Seems like you are still a bit clumsy, Clarrie."

Clarissa waved her hand at the comment. "One, I'm not Clarrie anymore, and two, I'm not clumsy."

He sat up and gave her a look. "Well, I don't know what women call it these days but when you fell, I had to catch you. I don't think you did that deliberately. That makes you—"

She placed her hand on his mouth. "Stop talking. You're wasting brain cells. Are you okay?"

"Ow! You're still the same."

"Listen, this never would have happened if you had just moved out of the way. So the fact that you wound up on the ground is bad but not tragic." She stood up and wiped down the sides of her dress.

"Are you going to get up or are you going to lay there waiting for sympathy or the press?"

His gave her a full-fledged smile, and she was stuck in place. Bain Parcel had been blessed from birth with good genes. His smile was enough to make a woman think twice about whatever it was she was thinking.

He kept eye contact with her and got to his feet. He brushed off his jeans and leaned over and picked up his hat. He dusted the hat off and then tipped it at her. "Thank you for your concern."

He leaned in, and for a moment, Clarissa thought he might kiss her in the middle of the street.

"Clarissa Hastings, are you okay?"

Clarissa didn't realize until that second that she was leaning into the kiss with Bain. She snapped herself back and then straightened herself up.

"Thank you, Geeta, I'm well," Clarissa said, keeping her hand next to her side so she didn't push Bain back down on his backside.

Geeta was the owner of the town hangout called the Banter House. Geeta was well-intentioned and not a gossip, but Clarissa couldn't chance anyone knowing there was any connection between her and Bain.

Bain raised his hand." She's fine. I've got her."

Clarissa plastered a smile on her face and took a step back onto Bain's foot. She heard him grunt as she nodded towards Geeta.

"I've got this."

Geeta turned and walked away. When Clarissa faced

Bain, he still had that same silly smile on his face. Instead of him being angry, it seemed like he was amused.

"I can see you're a woman who knows how to use her heels to their best advantage."

"I do, and I also know how to use my knees."

Bain took a step back. "Fortunately, I don't need that kind of help. I'm glad that I was here to help you when you fell."

"Fell!" She wanted to stamp her feet in frustration, but instead, she took a deep breath and smoothed the sides of her dress and then stood, straightening up.

"Okay, have it your way! Do whatever you want; just go away."

She kept her cool and calmly walked away even though she was so frustrated she could have run away from him screaming. She had to keep her cool and make sure he knew that he didn't move her at all.

She was over Bain Parcel. She just had to remember that those eyes could woo anyone and mean nothing. His lips never told the truth. Besides, beauty didn't guarantee happiness; she of all people could attest to that. She had fallen once, but she wouldn't fall twice. Bain could go back to wherever he came from. She wasn't going to be the small town stopover.

Clarissa had built herself up so she could take care of herself. She had invested well, gone to school and educated herself, and then she decided to stay in the town where she could look after the people she cared about. She didn't need Bain. She didn't want Bain.

"Clarrie?"

When he said her name in those deep tones, the sound wrapped her up in thoughts of nights by a fireplace, long talks, and walks on the beach.

She didn't even bother to turn around. "Yes?"

"I know you want me to go but I can't. I came for you."

Spinning on her heel, she took her finger and poked his chest.

"You can go back to wherever you came from. There's nothing between us anymore."

"I disagree, Clarrie."

"Oh, can you get it through your head that what's done is done? And don't call me Clarrie; that's not my name!"

Bain took a step closer to her and flashed her a wide grin before running his hand down her cheek.

"You are still full of fire, and you're still the most beautiful woman I've ever met."

The words wrapped around her heart, and she could feel that dreamy sensation washing over her and the slight sway towards him.

"My Clarrie."

The name was like a bucket of cold water being splashed on her.

"Your Clarrie? I don't think so, and I'm sure by now you've met lots of beautiful women since you weren't with me so I'll take that compliment and go on my way."

"Before you go, I wanted to tell you something."

Clarissa was confused and shook her head, looking at him.

"What?"

"I'll be seeing you later, Mrs. Parcel," he said, whispering in her ear.

She grabbed his forearm and tugged him close.

"What are you, crazy! I'm not that anymore," she hissed.

His grin was so wide she could see every one of his perfect white teeth.

"If you had answered any of emails, letters, or correspondence, you would have known. Our divorce never went through. We've been married the whole time. I know you need time to process this, and I'll make sure to give it to you, but I wanted you to be aware because I'm in town for Adam's wedding."

Clarissa waved it off. "Of course you are. The two of you have always been as thick as thieves."

"Well, Adam has asked me to be his best man, and I said yes."

"So, this matters to me because?"

"I'll have my wife on my arm when I walk down his aisle."

"You've got to be—"

Bain leaned in and placed a quick kiss on her lips.

"I know this is sudden, so we'll talk later. I rented a house in town so I'll be seeing you, Mrs. Parcel."

She watched him get into his car and pull away. She had to let him go. She couldn't kill him on the street. It was as if he hadn't left. She was feeling the tug of attraction and frustration. Bain Parcel was the football king, and the one everyone wanted. When he chose her, he made her believe she was more than a pretty face. Then she grew up. Mrs. Parcel? He had to be wrong. Those were the words that played in her mind as she walked down the street.

It wasn't true. She wasn't Mrs. Bain Parcel. The first break up had sent her into a tailspin; to do it again might break her.

Two

Bain stood in the office and waited for his reckoning to come. Everything had a price. He'd worked on this speech several times. He thought he had imagined everything that could be thrown at him.

Now he was standing in the home office of his best friend, Adam Cade. He needed his help to get back something that was priceless. If there had been any other way to get what he needed, he would have taken it. He knew Adam had his back. They had gone to school together, left town to find their way in the world together, and served as the reality stick when their lives had taken off, and both of them had started making money. Even with all of that, it wasn't until he had caught a fever and confessed his secret to Adam during his feverish delirium. He had married the beauty queen Clarissa, his one true love, and he had divorced her via proxy six months later.

Bain's family didn't have the deep roots Clarissa's had. They had moved to Sweet Blooms to raise him, and when he left on his "football" career, they had left as well to travel. He knew they'd wanted a child and sacrificed to have him. After pouring eighteen years of love and affection into him, they pulled up their roots and moved to a gated community. After twelve years of traveling the world and becoming the face of fitness for who don't want to become a bodybuilder but still want to look toned, he had decided to take his dad's advice. His dad had told him when he felt it was time to go, don't second guess your gut. Move on to the next adventure in life. Only he didn't want a new career. Money wasn't an issue for him, so the thing he really wanted was the woman he loved…if she would have him.

Bain realized this wasn't a sure thing, and the decision to come back to the only woman he loved may have sounded great in books, but he wasn't so sure Clarissa would think so. He had known Clarissa while he lived in Sweet Blooms. They had been friends even. When he left on scholarship, they had stayed in touch. Then, five years ago, he came to visit Clarissa, and he saw his best friend and the woman he trusted with his heart. They got married, and he went back on the road with the football team. Two months later he got injured, and football was over. Instead of running to his friend, he stopped calling her and wouldn't take her calls.

Adam walked into the office. Bain could tell he was braced for the bad news.

"Stop tensing, Adam. I haven't even said what I want yet."

"Bain, the only time you want to meet in an office is when it's about money, career, or harebrained schemes. Otherwise, we meet in bars like all men do."

In the room were two chairs with a small table in the middle. Bain gestured for Adam to take a seat.

"I won't beat around the bush. I want to get Clarissa back."

Adam sat back in his chair and ran his hand over his face.

"Here I was trying to figure out which one we would be addressing tonight—money, career, or harebrained schemes—and I see you've outdone yourself. We are talking about all three."

Bain leaned forward in the chair.

"Hear me out first."

"Bain, I don't think there is a plan good enough to make a woman forget you divorced her via proxy after you stopped talking to her."

"I know I have work to do—"

"Work? No, man, I don't think you understand. The Statue of Liberty needs work. Some of the stonework on Mount Rushmore needs work. The work you are looking at is the same kind of work it would take to push the continents together again."

"It's bad, but it's not that bad. Clarissa is the most logical person I know."

Adam snorted. "You should have offended the logical person, but instead, you scorned the woman who loved you. Game over!"

Bain reached out and grabbed Adam's forearm.

"Adam, I need your help. If there's any way… If it were you and Hannah, what wouldn't you try?"

Bain could see Adam swaying towards his side. Heaving a deep sigh, he asked the question that Bain had been waiting for: "Okay, what do you need me to do?"

Bain sat back and let out a sigh of relief of his own.

"I want to bring Clarissa as my date to your wedding."

Adam looked at him, blinked, and then slapped his leg as he laughed. He kept laughing until he realized that Bain wasn't laughing with him. Then he stopped and started to shake his head in denial.

"Adam—"

"Brother, find another way."

"I don't see it!"

"Well, keep looking! Do you understand what you are asking? Hannah doesn't like Clarissa!"

"Clarrie can be challenging," Bain agreed.

"When I first got here, Clarissa hit on me. I knew it didn't mean anything, but Hannah didn't, and now you want me to tell my fiancée that I'm adding a person she dislikes to the wedding party?"

"Adam—"

"Stop right there. You are groveling at the wrong doorstep. This is what I'll do for you. Hannah is up at the house. I'll send her to you. Whatever she says, I'll do."

Bain heard the finality of Adam's decision in his voice, and he nodded.

If waiting for Adam to come into the office was hard, waiting for Hannah was making him sweat. It seemed like it took her an hour or two, but Bain knew it wasn't more than fifteen minutes.

"Hey, Bain, what's up? Adam said you wanted to talk to me."

Bain looked at her happy face and wide grin. He knew strategy from football, and today he would have to use some of it.

"Hannah, I'm in love, and I need your help getting the girl."

"Who's the lucky girl?" she said as she took a seat in one of the chairs.

"My wife."

"Oh!" she said with raised eyebrows. "Well, that's a new one. I would think one of the top models would have no problem wooing his wife."

"Life is never as easy as it seems. Let's say we've had some misunderstandings and I thought she needed some time to get over it. In retrospect, that might not have been the best answer."

Hannah reached out and patted his hand.

"I completely understand how misunderstandings and doubt can get in the way of a relationship. Is she in town?"

"She lives in Sweet Blooms."

Hannah sat back in the chair. "Really? Who?"

Bain took a deep breath and let it out.

"Clarissa."

He saw all of the sympathy he had built drain out of her face.

"You're better off without her. Besides, I hate to tell you this, but she goes after every single man." Hannah stood up and walked towards the door.

Bain didn't try to stop her; he just started talking.

"I told her for better or for worse, and when things got worse, I disappeared for six months, divorced her by proxy, and didn't talk to her for five years. She's a piece of work, but no woman deserves that," he said in a low voice.

Hannah had her hand on the door and stamped her feet.

She faced Bain and shook her head.

"Really, Bain! I'm not a fan of Clarissa's, but really? I think it's in my best interest to tell her not to listen to you."

Bain knew he had a sad grin on his face.

"You didn't know her before, but if you had, you'd know that I don't deserve her, but I love her, and I was stupid. I let my ego get in the way of our love. I may have a chance to make it better. Will you help me, Hannah?"

Hannah folded her arms over her chest and then sighed.

"Okay, what do you want?"

Three

Clarissa had a guilty pleasure. When she was stressed and needed some relief, she would go to a nearby ranch to go on a nice ride with a docile horse. The amount of concentration it took for her to keep the horse on the trail allowed her to let all of the other thoughts go and give her some relief. Today she had a docile mare called Goldy. True to her name, her coat looked golden in the morning sun.

"It's time for the both of us to get a little lost in the trail. What do you think, Goldy?" she asked.

The mare looked at Clarissa as she mounted, and that was all the confirmation she needed to begin the ride.

The sun was up, but the heat hadn't begun. There was still a hint of a breeze to keep her cool in between the gaps in the trees. She hadn't bothered to bring a hat. She wanted to have the full effect today. She wanted to be grateful for what she had and think about what could have been or what was. This ride would center her.

The mare had taken just a few steps out of the enclosure when she saw a large speckled stallion trotting down the trail. Bain Parcel was sitting atop the stallion as if he had been born on it.

"Are you starting your ride?" he asked as if they were friendly neighbors. "Can I ride with you?"

She looked at him, and the words flew out of her mouth before she could stop them.

"No! I'm out here to get away from you!" Then, as if she realized the words had escaped, her hands flew over her mouth a minute too late.

Bain laughed.

"Some things never change. Your temper is a work of art sometimes, Clarrie. But in all the time I've known you, I've never known you to run from anyone or thing."

She knew he was baiting her, and still, she had no way to stop it.

"Fine, fine, do what you want. Come on the trail with me, just don't ruin my peace." She flicked the reins, and Goldy took off with her mellow gait. Normally, with each step, Clarissa's thoughts would fade away, and she'd lose herself in the slow gait. Today with each step, her mind wandered to her quiet companion. Was he cool enough in those black jeans? The jeans made him look like he had to be lifted to be put on the stallion. She didn't think he could even walk or be comfortable. She didn't hear a word from him. The only thing that broke the silence was the clip-clopping of the horse's shoes. When a breeze came by, she tilted her head to the wind and wondered if he was cool enough in that white shirt with the rolled-up sleeves. When had his arms gotten so big?

"Clarrie, if your back gets any stiffer, you will break. Stop thinking and ride," he said as he pulled the stallion next to her. "I hope I'm not the reason you don't seem to be enjoying the ride."

"No. You? Please. I have other things to think about."

She couldn't seem to find them or even remember them, but she was sure she had other things to think about.

"Good," he said as the horses synced their steps.

"Do you really expect me to relax while you are riding next to me?"

"Is riding next to me a problem? Do I smell?"

She looked at him incredulously.

"You don't smell as you well know. I just don't like to look at you."

"Am I ugly?"

She pursed her lips and looked at him.

"What is it? Are you at the age where you need confirmation of your looks? You still look amazing, Bain."

"It's like yesterday. I'm just trying to be present to—"

"Let's not bring up yesterday when you caused me to fall."

"You mean when I broke your fall."

She sucked her teeth and sat straighter in the saddle to speed the horse up. "Yesterday is over, and there's no sense in arguing about it."

"I wouldn't want there to be any misunderstandings between us."

Clarissa took a deep breath and looked at Bain. This was maybe day two of seeing him, and already he was getting under her skin. When she looked at him, she could almost forget what he had done and look at him as her bestie. He had been that before he had abandoned her.

She faced forward and didn't speak. She could feel the heat forming behind her eyes. She wouldn't cry. Clarissa was grateful the horse had walked this trail for years and now needed little to no direction to stay on the main path. Normally she would have gone on the less-traveled path to avoid people, but today she was going where Goldy wanted to go.

"It's like old times when we—"

"Stop! Let's stop right there. We don't talk about old times."

"Were they all bad?"

"Bain, is that why you came back to Sweet Blooms? Are the memories something you've come to relive?"

"I came for Adam and Hannah's wedding. I'm the best man. I wouldn't be telling the whole truth, though, if I told you I didn't think about you."

"Stop doing that. It's not helpful for you."

"Adam's wedding is the talk of the town. Do you want to go with me?"

"I have to say I have no clue how to respond to that. Should I push you off of your horse or just ignore the request?"

"Clarrie, I'm asking you to be my date."

Clarissa heard him and just kept her eyes forward.

"I'm sure you think you're doing me a favor, but you're not. I don't want to date you. Bain, let's put all of our cards on the table. Why are you here?"

He gave her a small smile.

"I'm here to get you back."

Clarissa gave him a double look and then led her horse to the side of the trail where she dismounted. When Bain had followed and was standing in front of her, she spoke.

"You have been traveling so long you think you can do anything. I don't care what you want. I don't want you, Bain."

"I messed up. I did it all wrong."

She tied Goldy to a bush and went to sit on a nearby boulder. She waited for him to follow her to the boulder. When he was standing in front of her, she started.

"What is it? Do you need a new thrill? Do your regular groupie girls or whatever not do it for you?"

"It's not that."

Clarissa looked at Bain and waited for the explanation. She wanted to understand why the only man she had ever loved, who had abandoned her, was back.

"Bain, talk to me."

"I messed up, Clarrie. I have money, and I'm going to leave modeling."

Clarissa gave him a look. "Okay, that doesn't answer the question on why Sweet Blooms."

"You're the only woman I've ever loved."

It was funny to hear him say the words. Clarissa could remember waiting in her house for the phone to ring. Hoping each time she went to the mailbox she'd get something from him. Now, five years later, he was here.

"You don't know how long I waited for those words, and now they're just words."

Bain looked away and ran his fingers through his hair.

"Do you feel anything for me?" he asked in a low voice.

Clarissa looked at him from the boulder.

"I'll always love you, Bain, but right now I just can't trust you."

With that, she got up, mounted Goldy, and then pushed her to trot back to the shed at the end of the trail. When she dismounted, she gave the reins to the hand who was in the overhang and went to her car. She had to wait a moment for the tears to fall; after they did, she was able to see.

Bain Parcel had said he loved her, again. She wanted to trust him, but her heart was still cautious.

Four

The Sweet Blooms committee threw a business luncheon for the business owners twice a month. With all of the new developments going on, the party served as a way for everyone to get together and voice any concerns they may have. It started with a meeting and ended with a buffet.

During the buffet, she avoided owners who tried to pushed their agenda and took the time to observe what everyone was doing. She always wound up being at a table by herself, and she usually preferred it.

An hour in, the only people who were left were the new, the desperate, and the late. In Clarissa's view, these were the more interesting people in the town. It was also the easiest way to see who was new and what was on the horizon. Today she wasn't focusing on the crowd as much as she usually did. The reason was Bain Parcel.

He'd shocked her with his declaration, and she'd shocked herself by telling him the truth about her feelings. He still had the ability to make her forget herself and speak her thoughts. What she discovered yesterday was that no matter how much time had passed, there was still a part of her that still had feelings for him.

If the rumor mill was true, he was here for the first of many Sweet Blooms weddings. She had to find a way to deal with him. Clarissa needed to get her heart in check and let her logic take control of the situation.

If she itemized his characteristics, she could think of them academically. Bain was handsome by anyone's standard. He was taller than her, and that was part of the reason she felt safe in his arms. He was well built and could be useful when it was time to move things around. Not to mention, he could be the most thoughtful person ever. He was. Clarissa stopped. Her itemization wasn't going the way she thought it would, and it definitely wasn't making it easier to resist Bain.

Looking up from the table, she saw the focus of her thoughts manifest in front of her. Bain walked into the luncheon, and it was as if there was a collective breath taken. He smiled at a couple of board members and then did a sweep of the room until his eyes landed on her. He didn't come over like she thought he would. Instead, he went to the buffet and began to speak to some of the business owners.

Each person he talked to was enthralled by him, and she hated to admit she was too. He didn't try to be more, he just was. Sure, he had the face and the body of a model, but there was more. Something Clarissa could only define as Bain.

After she watched him talk to a couple of other people and take a seat at a table, she went to join him. She was never a person to run from a problem, and she wouldn't start now. When she was a couple of feet away, Bain looked up from his plate, his gaze meeting hers.

He made no move to greet her or give her the smile he had given the others; he just waited until she took a seat.

"I didn't know you were opening a business."

"As many merchants that will be involved with the wedding, it's almost the same."

Those eyes sucked her in and stripped her bare. Her clothes were her armor, but without any indications from him on how he felt, she was unsure and shifted in her seat nervously.

"So you're staying for the wedding?"

"Yes. Have you reconsidered and decided to go with me?"

Clarissa cleared her throat and looked around the room to see if anyone was nearby. As if they all knew this was an A-B conversation, no one came to sit at the round six-person table.

"Why would I do that?"

Bain smiled. "I'm good looking, and we make a formidable pair?"

Clarissa smiled. "You always did have a sense of humor."

"I'm serious. Come with me to the wedding."

"I don't think you've vetted this request with Hannah. I can assure you I'm the last person she wants to have at the wedding and definitely not in her wedding party."

Bain got up and took a seat right next to Clarissa.

"Come on, Clarrie, do you think I'd invite you unless I already knew you'd be welcome? I've dropped a lot of balls, but I've never taken you somewhere you'd be uncomfortable." She was stuck between the deep rumble of his voice next to her ear and the words he was saying.

"Bain, I-I don't think it would look right, and I have to live here when you're gone and—"

Trying to break the spell his voice was weaving, she sat back and looked at him.

The corner of his mouth turned up. "Which part would be inappropriate?"

"They'll be rumors I was throwing myself at you."

"Do you care?"

"I may come close to breaking the rules, but I don't cross the line. I'd be a gold digger for sure if I went with you."

"I don't remember you ever being concerned about what people think, Clarrie."

"It all changes when your husband divorces you, and you become the talk of the town."

"I think I can help that," he said with a smile.

"Can you change history? Can you take back the snide remarks they said when you left?" As soon as the words were out of her mouth, she wanted to kick herself. Bain lifted her chin and looked in her eyes.

"I can't change what happened, but I can change what they thought."

"What? What is it that you think you can say to change all of their thoughts, oh great one?" she said sarcastically.

He held his hand up so she could see the gold band on his finger.

"Wait until they find out I didn't divorce you and you're still my wife."

Bain leaned in and kissed her on the cheek.

"I've got to go and talk about some press stuff with my agent, but as soon as I'm free, I'll explain it all."

Clarissa watched him walk out of the room, saying

goodbye to everyone as he passed. There were no words to describe how she felt. Someone touched her on the shoulder, and out of habit, she plastered a smile on and nodded every so often. As soon as she could, she walked away. The only thought she had was to get to the safety of her house.

She thought the problem would be adjusting to seeing Bain, but if he was telling the truth, she was still Mrs. Bain Parcel. She didn't know if she should laugh hysterically or plot a way to kill him; either way, she would do it in the privacy of her home.

Bain had been dreading this meeting since he came to town. When he had told his agent that he was retiring from modeling and taking a vacation, the silence had been deafening. After several hours on the phone, he had agreed to finish out his contracts for the year, but he wasn't signing any new ones.

Roger was his agent, and he had told him to take some time and go home. "Go to the wedding if you want, but let's not make any formal announcements until we talk about it." It had been two weeks since that conversation, and Roger was now coming to Sweet Blooms to talk. He decided to have the meeting in his rented home. He knew what Roger would see when he arrived. A small two-bedroom house that was probably as big as the living room in his house in California. He would look at the drapes and see they were handmade and matched the table cloth on the round wooden table. The layout of the house was pretty open as if someone built a room and then put the walls in last.

The floor was original wood floorings, and the house was decorated suspiciously. Almost like the realty office suggested the realtor let his wife do the décor as Ms. Atkins did at her husband's realty office. All in all, it was cozy and made him feel like he had a home.

It was 10:30 on the dot, and the doorbell rang. Roger nodded at him and then walked into the house. Bain smiled. Like clockwork, Roger looked around the place like he was an appraiser. Bain wished Clarrissa could be here. If Roger met her, he'd understand everything Bain loved about Sweet Blooms. The people weren't perfect, but they were true. Clarissa was smart, beautiful, and resilient. She had a giving soul that very few saw the depths of, and she had a way of finding those in need and helping them out without making them feel they were in debt.

Roger cleared his throat and faced Bain.

"Well, you did tell me it was homey."

Bain smiled and watched Roger pick a spot on the couch, inspecting the cushion before he sat down. Roger was in his late thirties and considered a catch in his industry. Like Bain, he was a hard worker. Often people didn't take him seriously with his blond hair and natural curl. He worked out at the gym. Bain knew because they used to work out together, but Roger never bulked up; he said it would cost him too much to get his tailored suits redone. Today he had on a polo and khakis. Bain knew as far as Roger was concerned, he was super casual. Bain took a seat, and Roger began.

"So, I can see you've had some time to see the people, and I think there was a sign when I was driving in about the wedding of the century happening in Sweet Blooms."

Bain nodded. "Adam Cade is getting married."

"Well, you should know you are in that picture too as part of the wedding party. So if you were trying to stay low and out of sight, you failed miserably. In fact, I've gotten more requests to sign you up and interview you."

Bain sighed. "Adam is my best friend, but I can see how no good deed goes unpunished. Adam wanted all the star power he could get to show off Hannah."

Roger smiled. "How quaint. I thought you needed a break because you were feeling like you weren't in the game anymore, but you can see from the requests you are, so when are you coming back to work?"

Bain tried to hide the smile that was itching to get out. He'd seen Roger pull this tactic with others. "You might be able to fast-talk those others but not me. I'm not on vacation. I'm leaving the game."

"I've got some things you can look at and… What did you say?"

"I said no. I know it's a word you're not used to hearing, but there it is."

Roger sat back on the sofa.

"What is it, Bain? Are you depressed? Do you need some help? I don't understand?"

Then Bain did laugh. Bain reached out and clapped Roger on the back.

"I'm not sick, Roger. I'm here to get the woman I love back."

Roger looked at him as if he were crazy and then shook his head.

"Oh, my friend, you are wrong. You are sicker than you know. Love brings us all down."

Five

Roger had stayed for two hours trying to convince him that love was a lost cause. When Roger left, he thought the best way to burn off some of his frustration was going for a drive and getting the lay of the land—how the town was setup. Instead of going to the heart of the town, he found himself headed for the courthouse where the board members had offices.

He knew Roger wanted him to stay and that he was income to him, but Bain wanted him to understand that he was a person. It didn't matter if he decided to stay in the game or not; he still needed this time to do something for himself. He wasn't an object to be talked over and around. He had paid his dues, invested wisely, and now it was time for him to take the same tenacity that had made him a great model and put it towards Clarissa.

"Why didn't Roger get it?" he muttered, frustration lacing his voice. He found himself at the light and looked at the sign that said *parking for community board events here.* He pulled into the driveway and went upstairs to see Clarissa.

Moments later, he stepped off of the elevator to see

Clarissa standing in the doorway of her office. A young woman was sitting at the desk, hero-worship in her eyes, watching Clarissa talk to a very large man. Bain didn't approach them, but he was close enough to hear.

"Ms. Hastings, I think you would find it would be a great asset to us all if you would endorse our business. The restaurant is vegan and organic, and you'd be an asset," said the round man as he leaned expectantly towards Clarissa.

"Mr. Patridge, I understand you need some representation, but I don't think I'm the one. I'm not vegan, nor do I particularly like organic."

"Yes, but a woman of your stature—"

Clarissa held up her hand. "Mr. Patridge, I'm a plain-spoken woman. If you are thinking my figure will convince others to try your place, then what you are looking for is a model, not a business endorsement. This board hasn't endorsed your place because you have yet to get a health code rating above a B."

The round man huffed and then ran his hands along his lapels as if he had to hold on to them to walk. "Well, Ms. Hastings, I think that's a bit judgmental. The health codes are very strict, and we're vegan, so some of those codes are too stringent."

"Let me stop you there. I review those codes quarterly. Mr. Patridge, let's not waste my time. I won't endorse a business I don't have confidence in. Spend your time getting up to code and less time schmoozing, and you may find your business will pick up. Now, good day."

As Mr. Patridge left, Clarissa and her assistant spotted him. The young lady said something to Clarissa, and she gave her a look of disapproval. There was nowhere to go, so Bain went forward to meet them.

"Hello, you're Bain Parcel. I'm Ms. Hastings' assistant," the young lady said, holding her hand out. I'm Jessica Lintel, an intern. It's nice to meet you. I've seen all of your shoots."

Bain smiled. "It's nice to meet you too."

Jessica was all of seventeen if she were a day, with curly black hair and brown eyes. She was short, barely up to Clarissa's shoulder, and she still had that shy air about her. Every so often, she looked back to Clarissa for a slight nod of encouragement.

"The newspaper says you are staying for the wedding of Adam and Hannah," Jessica said.

"I am."

"The rehearsals will be starting soon. Who are you taking to the wedding?"

When no one spoke, Jessica rushed in. "The girls at my school say you're going to bring that Italian model with you."

"I hate to disappoint them, but no, I won't be bringing Natalya." He looked at Clarissa who was getting that stiff back and distant look.

"Oh, that's a shame. Hot Topic magazine said you two were getting married," she rushed on.

"No, I couldn't if I wanted to. I'm already married."

Clarissa stood by Jessica, listening to her fan-like infatuation spill into her conversation with Bain. Bain was nothing if not courteous and polite. If she hadn't known the tell-tale signs of Bain being unhappy, she would have discounted the whole conversation.

She was still reeling from his declaration this

morning, but seeing him try to handle Jessica gave her a glimpse of what his life was really like. He said he was here because he still loved her, but was this just a phase for him? Not that she was taking anything he said seriously enough to change her life, but she still wondered. For the man who seemed to have it all, why look back at a wife he had in the very least tried to divorce. She knew the only one who had those answers was Bain.

The questioning was pretty much what she expected, and then he dropped the marriage surprise on Jessica. Thank goodness the phone rang and Jessica reluctantly excused herself to answer it.

"It's almost lunchtime. How about I meet you at Banter?"

He nodded. "In our booth?"

She hesitated. She shouldn't encourage him in any way, but she found herself nodding yes. "Yeah, in our booth."

About an hour later, Clarissa found herself walking in the front door of The Banter. It was one of the few places she could go and relax. On top of that, Geeta, the owner, was always trying to fatten her up and brought her mini desserts to die for.

She waved at the hostess and caught Geeta's eye when she came in the front door.

"He's here," she called out.

Both she and Bain liked Banter House, and she went to "their booth." When they first started coming here, they used to sit in the front so he could watch whatever car he drove down, but then they would constantly be disturbed by football fans who knew him. To avoid that, they picked a booth in the back, and he would tip a server to watch his car.

When she went down the walkway to see him, she could feel the anticipation building in her stomach. When he saw her, he stood up and held out his hand. He was still picture perfect. A perfect gentleman to his core and his manners made him all the more attractive to her. She knew she was conflicted about Bain. Today she had on a light pink dress. On the one hand, it made her look amazing because it was a wrap-around dress, but she didn't want to examine her choice of clothing because she hunted for this dress. Pink was Bain's favorite color on her. She put her hand in his and Bain gave it a gentle squeeze.

"Please," Bain said and motioned for her to take a seat in the booth.

His manners were always an attractive thing to her. She felt his hand guide her to the seat as if it was a warm brush that guided her along her back. Bain's touch. It was the reassuring touch of *I've got this* that made her all giddy.

After they were settled in their seats, a young waitress came by. She only had eyes for Bain. Before she could even speak, Geeta came over.

"Off with you, girl! They have no time for your foolishness," she said. Geeta was a rotund Indian woman who always had a smile and her hair in a top knot. "These young women. I have no time for them. Now you two I haven't seen in a minute. You two been hiding?"

"No, just trying to catch up," Clarissa said, giving Bain a look.

Geeta looked at Bain and tsked.

"Boy, I thought you had some sense. All that time you were bringing her here, and then you married her. I thought it was done."

Clarissa looked between Geeta and Bain.

"Well, then he left me—divorced me actually—so so much for that."

Geeta waved it off.

"If I left my Jerry for every stupid thing he did, I'd be leaving him every week."

Confused, Clarissa looked at Geeta "But—"

"Girl, you're young, and the boy still has his pride. I can't wait for you all to find your common sense. I'll get the regular for you both and make sure you're not disturbed."

Bain laughed. "It's nice to know that some things don't change."

Watching her walk away, Clarissa shook her head in agreement.

"Geeta will always be Geeta."

When their food and drink were delivered, Clarissa started with the obvious.

"I could see Jessica's questions made you uncomfortable."

"I wasn't happy about it, but it seems like it was in line with the rest of my day. I met with my agent today."

"What is it? You must make him money. Every agent loves that."

"Well, I have investments and other things to sell, but he was concerned because I told him I didn't want to do any more modeling."

Clarissa sighed. "I can see how he might not have been thrilled."

"The problem is, he's known me for a while. He knows that the dates with women are fake, the press releases we do are for business, and that I can do other things beside model. Today, though, I got it coming and going that the only thing I'm good for is modeling or who I'm with. I thought coming back to where I started would make me be seen differently."

Clarissa took a drink of her lemonade and gave Bain a once over. "I think it's hard for me and everyone else to imagine you having the problem of people judging you. We look at your life and think, *he's got to be living the dream.*"

"Having money doesn't give you a perfect life. Besides, I can't turn away fans. I appreciate what they've given me."

Clarissa reached across the table and put her hand on top of his.

"You can be grateful without sacrificing yourself. If you don't set boundaries, how will other people set them?"

Bain sat back and nodded. "You're right."

Clarissa smiled. "I usually am, but it's nice of you to acknowledge it."

Bain placed his hand atop hers and gave a squeeze.

"We need to talk."

Clarissa knew this moment was coming, and still, she wasn't sure she could deal with it.

"Bain, I don't know what happened or why you think we're still together but——"

"Clarrie, please let me talk."

Clarissa looked at him and nodded.

"When we were married, I was in my seventh year of football. I wasn't going to be a star in the game, but the money was good, and I enjoyed it."

Clarissa looked at him, confused. "I know that, and I didn't have a problem with you being a football player."

"The last time we saw each other, I went to play a game and then I'd come back. I injured myself in the game. They told me I could never play again. I panicked, and I stopped talking to you while I got all of the expert opinions and views."

Clarissa pulled her hand back and looked at him.

"You didn't tell me," she whispered.

"I didn't want to believe it, and I was looking for another answer. Well, I didn't find it in sports. I accidentally found it in modeling. Then I was just too ashamed that I went from a football player to a model."

"So you let your pride divide us?"

Bain looked into her eyes and nodded. "I was a fool. When you came the last time and saw me modeling with Natalya, I thought you were disgusted with me modeling, so I wanted to give you your freedom, and I sent the divorce papers."

Clarissa listened to how her dream unraveled. She listened to how she had suffered these last five years from foolishness. There was anger that came over her and then sadness. Deep sadness over time lost and love discarded.

"So what happened with the divorce papers?"

Bain shrugged. "I switched lawyers when I went from football to modeling. He started it and then sent it over in a box. Recently, the office has started moving, so I went through those boxes and found the document in the box. It was signed but never filed."

Clarissa took another sip of her lemonade and let it settle in. She felt like she was being hit a hundred miles an hour with new things so quickly she couldn't process it.

She cleared her throat.

"Well, if it's any consolation to you, I wasn't upset by your new career choice. I was upset that you hadn't spoken to me in six months and when I came to see you, you were in the arms of a younger woman taking pictures and smiling. I thought she was my replacement. When I calmed down and saw you were still together, I figured she was the reason you wanted a divorce."

"Natalya? She's a baby sister if anything. She helped me make some contacts, and we're friends, that it."

They finished their meal in silence.

"Well, Bain, maybe it was best it all ended the way it did. It seems like neither one of us trusted the other enough to love each other."

Bain paid the check, and then they walked out of the restaurant.

"I'm going back to work. I'll see you."

"Clarrie, you know everything. I need you to think about us. I messed up. I can't go back, but I never stopped loving you. I'm asking for another chance."

She was going to give him all the reasons why it wouldn't work. Then, before she could start on the laundry list that was in her head, he leaned in and kissed her.

"Don't give me the reasons why it won't work. Think on it," he whispered into her ear and then walked away.

She should be able to turn and go to work. Right now, her body was in overdrive. The place where he kissed her on the cheek was still warm from his contact. Even after everything she'd heard, she was still attracted to the man and in love with the boy. Bain was right; she couldn't tell him a thing now. She needed time to think about what to do with her new husband.

Six

The week was full of surprises. When Clarissa received a lunch invite from Hannah, she called her to make sure it wasn't a mistake. Sure enough, here she was in Banter watching Hannah take a seat in the booth she was at.

"Hi Clarissa, I know this invite was sudden, but I called Daisy to join us since she's in the wedding party as well. You don't mind, do you?"

Clarissa saw Daisy approaching the booth with her blonde hair, complete with flowers, piled atop her head.

"Of course not. She brings the flowers to the courthouse," Clarissa said. "She's also just started a joint venture with Patrick." Clarissa could see Hannah's eyebrow raised. Clarissa waved her expression away. "I do other things in town for others sometimes."

"I didn't know you kept track of those kind of things."

"It seems we are learning new things about each other," Clarissa said.

As Daisy got closer to the booth, Clarissa saw she had two bundles of flowers.

"Hi everyone! I'm so excited about the wedding.

I brought you both gifts," she said as she scooted Hannah over in the booth. Daisy had recently fallen in love with Patrick. The both of them were working the land and trying to make a new life. Patrick had come to town to sell his land, but now he was working on making the land work for him. He had the perfect partner with Daisy at his side; she was the florist and local herbalist.

"How are you and Patrick, Daisy?" Clarissa asked. "Have the two of you decided on what you're going to plant on the property?"

"It's amazing! I wanted to thank you for helping Patrick get the money he needed to pay his old debt. Now he's learning how to be a farmer. We're moving toward building a greenhouse to expand the flowers and herbs that I'm growing to the more sensitive herbs," she said with a smile that belied her happiness. "I'm sorry I was running late. I have a new worker— Joshua's aunt is starting—and I'm doing training little by little. She's great."

"No, we haven't been waiting long," Hannah said. "I'm curious to see if Clarissa will eat at all. I can't imagine much goes in with a shape like that."

"I think I'm about to surprise you. I eat all the time, and anything I want," Clarissa said with a smile.

Daisy laughed. "It's true. I've seen Clarissa eat, and she doesn't spare a fry."

Hannah looked between Clarissa and Daisy. "Well, I'm glad the two of you already know each other. Skye couldn't make it, but she already knows. You've been chosen to be in the wedding party."

Clarissa sat there and listened to Hannah. She knew she should tell her that she wasn't going to be part of the wedding party. She hadn't decided on what she was going to do, but if she were honest, she'd have to admit she wanted to be a part of the largest event in Sweet Blooms. She'd correct Hannah on her attendance later, but for now, she was enjoying what if felt like to be a part of the town and not an unofficial pariah.

Daisy reached across the table and broke Clarissa out of her reverie. "It's a wedding, don't worry. I've seen the color scheme, and I can assure you that it goes well with you."

"I don't think Clarissa has anything to worry about. If anything, I should make sure she doesn't outshine me."

"Hannah, you don't have to worry. What makes a bride shine is how much they love their fiancé and how much she's loved," Clarissa said.

Everyone at the table stopped, and Clarissa could feel their eyes on her. Daisy was smiling as if she had just won the lotto, and Hannah seemed shocked.

"Thank you, Clarissa, that is the nicest thing anyone has said to me about this whole wedding drama," Hannah confessed.

The next half an hour went by with Hannah explaining there would be more press than there were guests to the wedding. Adam's company was well known, and Bain was going to be there as well. The exposure was what the town wanted to use to highlight the other businesses. Cade was giving overboard in Hannah's opinion, letting the world know they were getting married.

Hannah's phone went off at the end of the lunch, and she looked around regretfully. "I'm sorry, guys, I've got to go. It seems like I have to approve the media list, and it's done by interview."

Hannah hugged Daisy and then reached out and tapped Clarissa's shoulder. "Thank you both for coming. I'll get back to you later."

Daisy waited until Hannah was gone, and then she turned toward Clarissa.

"So I heard there is something going on with you and Bain Parcel."

Clarissa almost choked on her lemonade. It never ceased to surprise her on how fast news went through Sweet Blooms—good, bad, or indifferent.

"Bain and I have known each other for a while. He's also bringing a lot of media attention and potential revenue to Sweet Blooms."

"He's been talking about you to the other guys in the wedding party. He told us you do charities for literacy and that you're a teacher. He seems to know a lot about you, and more importantly, he knows a lot more about you than anyone else," Daisy said, wiggling her eyebrows.

"So, is it true? Are you and Bain an item?"

"No," Clarissa replied with the quickness. "We're old friends. I don't know if you remember, but I was married to him, so yes, he knows me better than most people."

"Was married? I didn't know. I mean, you hear stuff in town, but it was always said that you two were dating and that it ended, but no one knew the details," Daisy said. Then Daisy reached out and touched Clarissa. "Are you going to be alright? I mean, I know the wedding is big news, but what about you?"

Clarissa could feel herself tearing up, and she smiled and took a deep breath.

"Thank you, Daisy. It's been a long time since someone asked me how I was. I'll admit I can easily remember why I married him in the first place."

Daisy sat back and looked at Clarissa.

"You don't have any of the anger tones when you talk about him. Is there a chance?"

"No!"

Daisy held her hands up. "You answered that one pretty fast."

"Ugh! It's hard to explain what happens between Bain and me."

Daisy laughed. "I imagine it's the same thing that happens when a lot of women look at him. They realize he is incredibly gorgeous and they just look at him for academic purposes, of course."

Clarissa groaned. "It's true. He's attractive."

Daisy smiled and waited.

"Okay, okay, you're right. He's still hot, and I'm not unaffected. But Bain and I have a history that is convoluted and crazy."

"It sounds like you and Bain have some work to do."

"Work?"

"Love is work. I don't know why they make it sound like it's a walk in the park, but what Patrick has definitely shown me and continues to do so every day is that to make love work, you have to work at it. Besides, I think you two look like one of those magazine power couples."

Clarissa looked at Daisy and shook her head. "You're sweet but don't get moonbeams and stars caught in your vision."

Daisy leaned over the table, moving closer to Clarissa, who met her halfway. "I don't have to have stars and moonbeams. I know you, Clarissa, and underneath that beautiful face you are an amazing woman any man would be happy to have."

The second surprise came the next day when Bain invited her to the media room. She had told him she wanted to talk and thought they would meet at Banter again. Instead, he invited her to the media room that had been set up on the Cade ranch.

"I thought this would look a lot more glamorous," Clarissa said, looking around the temporary shelter.

"Glamour isn't really part of the media." Bain showed her the different boards that were on the walls. "The days of flashing lights and people just showing up to events is over. It became too dangerous for the media and the people they were going to see."

"What are we talking about? A mob crush to get a picture?"

"Not always, but it used to happen. We're also talking about amateur media trying to harass a person or take so many flash shots the person being photographed or interviewed can hurt themselves getting away."

"I can see that it's hard to be glamorous on crutches."

He looked at her and patted his legs. "On top of that, my legs are insured for a million dollars apiece, so the more controlled the gathering, the less my premiums go up."

She followed him around the trailer as he explained the different boards that showed who was on the list to take pictures, where they were allowed to go, who had security to which sections, and who would have all-access passes. On one of the walls were even some questions that had been vetted to be asked.

She took a look at the questions board, and the one that jumped out to her was the question that asked if he was retiring and who his current love interest was.

Clarissa pointed to the board. "So these are the million-dollar questions?"

Bain smiled. "They're the ones I need to have an answer for, or my base will think I'm teasing them, so my agent says."

"I didn't realize that this wedding could affect your livelihood."

"I've made my decision about that."

"You're really going to walk away?"

Bain grinned. "I've already cut my ties with most of my old life. I have nothing waiting for me."

Clarissa looked around the room, and the question hung in the air. Did Bain have anything here waiting for him?

"Listen, one of the reasons I wanted to talk was to say I'll go to the wedding with you."

Bain stood up and went to her, but Clarissa stopped him with a look.

"I said I'm going to the wedding with you. I didn't say anything else."

"Thank you."

She extended her hand, and for a moment, she wasn't sure he'd take it. When his hand clasped hers, a sigh of relief went through her. The handshake wasn't long, but for that brief couple of seconds, she could feel the warmth of his hand and the zing of heat that spread through her body and settled in her stomach.

Realizing that this was part of the Bain effect, Clarissa took her hand back, and she told Bain what had happened between her and Hannah. When she was sure he was okay with her and Hannah, she left, thinking she didn't know what it was, but she was going to have to find a way to deal with the Bain effect if she was going to survive this wedding.

"Thank goodness you were available, and I'm so sorry I'm imposing," Cassandra Olsen said as she grabbed her car keys. "I don't know what we're going to do when we have a child."

Clarissa laughed. "It's no problem, and I'm sure you and Evan will have figured this all out before you have a baby."

"Babies. He's on babies, and I'm trying not to go crazy planning two weddings for us."

"Think on your wedding later; you've got to go to the fitters—"

"The fittings for these dresses. You wait until your arrives. You'll wonder if they ever took measurements. Okay, Nyx is in the back. He's asleep now, but if he wakes he can come out of his crate and—"

Clarissa folded her arms across her chest and then pointed towards the door. "Evan will be here shortly. I'll let him know where you went, and if Nyx wakes, I can assure you I know how to take care of your latest addition."

Cassandra grabbed Clarissa in a bear hug. "You are totally awesome. The town doesn't know what they're missing in you."

Clarissa pulled away. "On that note, out with you."

"I'm going, I'm going."

Clarissa watched Cassandra get into her vehicle

and drive off. She had gone back to her office after the media room tour. Then Cassandra told her the fitter had called, and she needed to go, but Cassandra and Evan had just bought a new puppy. They had decided it would stay with Cassandra while Evan finished building the house they would stay in as husband and wife. Nyx, the Great Dane puppy, couldn't be left alone at such a young age. Cassandra pleaded, and that was how Clarissa wound up puppy sitting until Evan came over.

She went to check on the puppy. Clarissa could see that Cassandra had put the crate next to the couch, and inside lay the sleeping puppy.

It was stretched out as if it didn't have a care in the world. Little did it know that it was so loved by two amazing people. Clarissa looked at the puppy, and tears came to her eyes. Once upon a time, she had thought she would have a relationship where she could be herself, and she would share a life with someone special, maybe even create a life.

After Bain, she started to believe what others had said about her. Her aunt had taken her in after the death of her parents in a car crash. Her aunt had told her she was too prideful and depended too much on her looks. When Bain hadn't returned, mean gossipmongers who had wanted Bain for themselves or had always disliked Clarissa said she was too uppity to have a man. The gossipmongers weren't many, but when a person is already down, there doesn't have to be a lot of people to make her fall all the way.

As the years had passed, she had put herself back together. She looked at families but didn't see herself with one in the future. She'd volunteered to help others and figured that was as close as she'd get. She was a teacher by trade, and she had thought Bain had been generous in his settlement with her. Now she realized she just always had access to his money.

When she'd decided to tutor Evan, she'd made the decision to help those who needed a little push. She helped a couple with a loan here. She'd gifted a contract there. It was never large until Daisy and Patrick.

The puppy stirred, and Clarissa watched Nyx snuggle into a tight ball. "Maybe that's what I need, a puppy.

She heard the jingle of keys and went back to the front door. Evan Sparrow walked in the door and saw her. His grin was infectious.

"Hi, Clarissa. As soon as I saw you, I thought, *am I late for class?*" He gave her a hug and then closed the door.

"Cassandra left and couldn't leave Nyx alone, so I agreed to be the temp help until you arrived."

"She's totally taken with the dog."

Clarissa gave him a light punch on his shoulder. "She better not hear you call Nyx a dog. Otherwise, you might be in a dog house because Nyx can't live in one of those. It's inhumane."

They both laughed. Clarissa used to tutor Evan Sparrow to help him learn to read. While he could build anything by eye, his personal mountain was literacy. Now he read several books a week.

"Is everything going good for you and Cassandra?"

Evan smiled. "Yes, mother hen, all your chicks are good. How about you?"

"Me?"

"Yes, there are words being thrown around about you and Bain."

"You know we have history, Evan, and that's not as easy to get over. I'm going to be in the wedding party, so I'll at least help him get past this media moment."

"And then?"

"It's funny; I was thinking about what I used to dream about. I was thinking that having a puppy is a great way for you and Cassandra to test the waters."

Evan sighed. "Well, you know I'm the last person to give advice. But what I will say is the most important thing is trust. Trust strengthens love. You've always been there to help me, and I can't tell you how grateful I am. Let me repay my debt with this truth I know about you. You deserve someone you can trust with your heart, and you shouldn't settle for less."

Seven

It had been a while since Bain had been to Clarissa's house. It was done in Clarissa's favorite color of blue. It was full of multi-functional furniture in the living room, and her kitchen was a bright yellow. Flowers were in flower boxes around the house and by every window.

Clarissa had called him and told him she needed to talk to him. He hadn't pushed her since she agreed to go to the wedding although it wasn't the kind of arrangement he had been looking for. The wedding was in another two weeks, so when she said she wanted to talk, he wasn't sure if it was to confirm the wedding or to cancel. Either way, he came to her house.

When he got out of his car, she was standing in the doorway.

"I'm sorry it was such short notice, but I'm happy you made it."

She stepped aside, and the smell of cookies wafted in the air. He passed her and went to the couch. After he had taken a seat, he looked at Clarissa and knew whatever this was it was important to her. Clarissa hadn't put on any makeup, and she was dressed in blue jeans and a white shirt.

"Clarrie?" he asked.

"I'm okay. I've been thinking, and I need to say some things to you. So take a seat, and we can try to get through this."

He didn't want to tell her he was already sitting or that she was asking him to do things he was already doing.

She sat down on the couch, then she stood up and began to pace in front of him.

"Clarrie?" he asked again. This time he was a little more controlled and looked for any sign of why she would be so nervous. "Are you hurt?"

Clarissa stopped and looked at him and let out a deep sigh. "I'm not, but I was, and maybe there's something left." She took a seat on the farthest point on the couch. He wanted to go to her and pull her into his arms, but this much nervous energy needed to be burned, and Bain still wasn't clear what the problem was.

"I wanted to tell you that I thought about you and me and everything and I've come to some conclusions," Clarissa said, her hand twisting in her lap.

"Okay, Clarrie, tell me what it is."

"I want to start at the very beginning and that way it will all make sense," she said. She looked up, and he nodded for her to go on.

"You know I'm from Sweet Blooms," she said. Her gaze kept flitting away from his. "My parents loved to travel and loved each other. They were on a trip, and it appeared that there was a mountain slide and I lost the both of them. My aunt, Temperance Thorne, took me in."

"I didn't know. She must have been devasted."

Clarissa sighed and folded her arm across her chest. "I suppose that's one way to look at it. She was a single woman who had decided early on never to have children. When my mother passed, she was still living in Sweet Blooms. There wasn't really an alternative. She wound up with a child she never wanted. Sibling rivalry was always strong between them, and when my mother died, I was the stand-in for every dispute that was never settled."

Bain looked at Clarissa, and a sense of deep regret filled his soul. "I take it this wasn't the ideal way to grow up," he said neutrally.

Clarissa shrugged. "It was very challenging. Temperance said I was an exact copy of my mother. If you saw my aunt, you wouldn't even know we were related. She would tell me that my mother had it easy in life and that she didn't love me. If she had, she wouldn't have left me."

Bain knew Clarissa was a sensitive woman. He couldn't imagine the little girl who had lost so much and then was with a guardian who, for all intents and purposes, was jealous of her and her mother.

"I'm so sorry, Clarrie."

"Thanks."

"Were you able to tell anyone?"

Clarissa shrugged. "Yes, it was hard, but I learned how to keep family business at home. While I appreciate your concern, I didn't tell you for the sympathy. I told you because I decided that I wouldn't settle for someone who didn't want to be with me or who thought I wasn't good enough. When we got married, I thought I had found someone who would value me and put me first."

Bain heard the words, and each one of them was a dagger to his heart. He knew she hadn't had a happy home life, but nothing like this. Now he thought about how his pride got in the way and how much he hurt her. He wasn't sure if he had damaged what could have been between them beyond repair.

"Sorry doesn't begin to make up for what happened between us. I—"

She stopped him with a sad smile. "I want to tell you that I think I've worked through my aunt and you, but the truth of it is, I think I'm working on it. After being in your media center, I understand that this wedding is really important, and because of that, I want to propose something to you that I think will work for us both."

Bain didn't say anything. Instead, he listened to what she said and let the words and the weight of what he had done to her sink in. He knew he was confident about what he wanted, but now he felt as though his plan to win her back was arrogant and inconsiderate. He would do whatever she asked. She deserved that. He was just happy she hadn't cut him out completely.

"What can I do?"

Clarissa sat down and looked at him with a smile on her face that was free of the tension he'd seen when he came in.

"I won't deny that I love you, Bain. I just won't short change myself to be with someone who can't trust me enough to tell me everything. I want to be on a team, not a side piece that has no say. So this is what I'm thinking.

I'll go to the wedding with you. We'll do what you need for the media. I don't want to have a negative impact on your career, and you've already told enough people that I can go with you no problem. After the wedding, you'll give me a divorce. I want the freedom to try to find someone else. I may leave Sweet Blooms. I don't know. What I do know is a friend of mine recently told me something that I'm going to take to heart. I'm not going to settle."

Bain waited, and when she didn't say anything else, he leaned forward.

"As usual, I can see that you've thought of what's best for you and me. I don't deserve it, but still, you thought about me and my career," he said.

Clarissa reached out and pushed an errant strand of hair from his forehead.

"When you love someone, you don't stop loving them because things go sideways. Besides, don't make me sound so altruistic. This wedding will give me the opportunity to be out and about in Sweet Blooms in a way I've never been. I think I need this to be me."

"Clarrie, you're killing me."

Clarissa stood up and walked to the door. "Don't give me your answer now. I want you to think about it. I want you to understand that when this wedding is done, we'll be done."

Bain looked at her and could see that now wasn't the time to talk about anything. In fact, after all, he had heard he needed time to think about what he was going to do and what would be best for Clarissa.

"To what do I owe the honor," Daisy said as Clarissa walked into the flower shop. Daisy was all smiles and anticipation as she watched Clarissa. "I went ahead and booked the shop just for us, and I've closed the shop per your request. I imagine this must be uberly important."

Clarissa had grown to be friends with Daisy as she worked with Patrick to help him secure his debt and get the funding to work the land he had inherited. Clarissa produced a box of desserts from the Sweet Blooms Cafe and put it on the counter between them.

"Wow, this must be serious if you went to get Bloom desserts," Daisy said as she opened the box and took a deep breath.

"It is." Clarissa looked at Daisy as she took a bite into a pastry and settled down. "I wanted to make sure you were open minded and happy before we had this conversation," she said.

Daisy took another bite and leaned back. "I am definitely in my happy place," she said in a sing-song voice. "I want you to know my mind is opened. Getting these pastries is the quickest way to heaven on earth."

Clarissa was glad she had bought the pastries and even happier that she had decided to talk to Daisy.

"Okay, tell me as the wave of euphoria is still upon me. What's going on?"

"It's Bain. You were right; I still have feelings for him."

Daisy opened her eyes and stared at Clarissa. "You remember what I said. Love takes work and not just for today."

Clarissa nodded. "I understand, but I'm not looking for long-term love. I'm looking to have some resolution in my life."

"Okay, and how do you want to get that resolution?"

Clarissa squared her shoulders and then looked her in the eye. "I told Bain I would go with him to the wedding and then I wanted to get a divorce that was real."

"What?"

"That's right, I didn't tell you. We were married. I thought we were divorced, but it turns out we're still married."

Daisy's mouth opened and closed like a fish out of water. "Hold up! You are telling me that right now you are married to Bain, and you made some weird deal with him to be his wife at the wedding, and then he'll divorce you?"

"Yes."

"That means right now you are Mrs. Bain Parcel?"

Clarissa nodded. "I am, but it's just Bain. He's a good man, but my trust levels are just sub-zero now. At any rate, this will be good for us both. I will go to the wedding, and he can get through that. Then I'll have some exposure being more social in Sweet Blooms, and then we can go our separate ways. What do you think?"

"I think this only happens in Sweet Blooms," Daisy said. "First, it doesn't matter what I think, or what anyone else thinks for that matter. What matters is that you are content with your decision. Now that I've given you that disclaimer, let me say something that I can say from personal experience.

A lot of things that I thought were important weren't all that important when I thought I would never see Patrick again. It doesn't mean that what happened in the past isn't an issue. What it means is that a person can't live in their past if they want to have a future."

Clarissa sighed. "I hear what you are saying, and I understand that I've been trapped in my past and that's what I'm trying to get out of now."

Daisy smiled. "I can see you've put a lot of thought into this. I have to say you are one of the smartest women I know, Clarissa. Trust yourself but be mindful; the heart rarely listens to the head."

"I think I'm past that problem," Clarissa said.

"Really, have you looked at him lately? You already said you still care for him. How hard would it be to stay his wife and work it out?"

"He hasn't said yes, and at the end of the day, the problem isn't if I love him. It's that I don't trust him to tell me everything."

Daisy popped another pastry into her mouth. "Out of curiosity, what would it take for you to trust Bain? You seem to have an idea in your head."

Clarissa pulled the box closer to her and took a whiff.

"I don't know. I think what I'd want is for him to share his feelings or, at the minimum, the things he's going through. I want to know if I ask he won't hide them."

Daisy licked her fingers after popping the last bite of the pastry into her mouth. "Love takes work. You want something? Don't expect him to be a mind reader. You want him to be open, so make sure you're just as open."

Clarissa sat back and looked at Daisy. "I hadn't given that any thought. Bain has always been so intuitive. So you don't think I'm crazy?"

"You're not crazy, so put that out of your mind. You made a decision. You put out a proposal, and now we wait. No matter what, you are still an amazing woman who is taking her own fate and healing into her own hands."

Clarissa smiled and picked up the last pastry in the box.

"Thank you for the encouraging words, but I want you to know that underneath all of this *I am woman hear me roar* façade, I'm not as sure as I look."

Clarissa had felt relieved when she left Daisy's the other day, but now she could barely keep her seat. Every time the phone rang, she grabbed it, hoping it was Bain. She took walks to distract herself from the wait. She knew several times Jessica had come into the office and tried to talk to her about upcoming events. Instead of giving her any feedback, she asked Jessica what her input was and to write it up so they could review it later.

Finally, the end of the day had come, and Jessica had left. Clarissa decided to try and do some work in her office. She would sign the documents Jessica said she needed to sign for tomorrow's meetings. Thank goodness they all had tags on them that said 'sign here.'

As if he was always there, Bain strolled into her office and sat in the chair in front of her desk.

"Do you have news for me?" she demanded. Waiting always made her cranky, and today was no different.

Bain smiled. "Yes, that would be my Clarrie. She doesn't like to wait for anything."

"I gave you time to think things over. I didn't think you'd take more than a couple of hours."

"I wanted to make sure I went over all of my options."

Clarissa gave him her full attention. "Options? I didn't realize I said there was anything that was negotiable."

"There is always room for negotiation as long as people are involved," Bain replied.

This wasn't the way Clarissa thought this would go. Already Bain was taking a situation she thought she had complete control of and twisting it.

"What's your answer?"

"I want to say yes with provisions."

Clarissa looked at him as if he had lost his mind. "Provisions?"

Bain chuckled. "Yes, you know it's when I give you what you want because I add things on that I want."

"I can't imagine what you'd want."

Bain leaned forward and looked her in the eye. "You, Clarrie. I want you."

Clarissa sat back and looked for any sign that he was joking or drunk.

"You seem like you are fine, but what you're saying makes no sense. I want a divorce."

"That's true. Today you want a divorce. I want to put in our little agreement that during the wedding we act like a real married couple. If at the end of it you still want to get divorced, I'll give it to you, but you have to be open to letting me try to win you back."

"Is this about your ego? Or is this some game for you? I don't understand."

Bain got up and went to kneel in front of her as she sat at the desk.

"Do you remember when I was on my knees before you last, Clarrie? It was to ask you to marry me. Not because of what you looked like or what others said. I was on my knees then, and I'm on my knees now because I love you. I've messed up. I've messed up in ways I didn't even know. I want a chance to make it right between us."

His voice was like silk, and it seeped into her and wove a delicate haze around her senses. There was a warmth to him that invited her to lean into him. She drew in a deep breath and took in Bain. This was all of her childhood dreams right before her. He couldn't realize how hard it was for her to resist. But this time she was going to do what was best for her heart and her soul.

She touched his jaw and relished in the feel of it. His jaw was firm, and when he closed his eyes, he looked like an angel in waiting. Then she snatched her hand back and sat back in the chair. When she sat back, his eyes flew open.

"You can try if you want to, but I don't think it will matter. Do what you want, but I'm still going to want that divorce."

Bain smiled. "We're playing for keeps, Clarrie."

"Do your best, Bain. Nothing will change."

"I want you to know that I don't plan on fighting fair."

"It's a waste, but do what you want."

Bain stood up and pulled her up with him.

"In case I don't get a chance to tell you later, I like you, and I respect you, Clarrie."

She nodded in acknowledgment. "You do now, but wait for it; I have a talent to annoy people."

He brought his hand up to her neck and then traced a finger down to her collarbone. She trembled beneath his touch and closed her eyes to let the feeling wash through her. She wanted to tell him that these touches didn't matter. It wasn't her body that wasn't sure; it was her heart. Clarissa opened her eyes to see Bain looking at her face in awe.

"This has never been a problem, Bain. I've never said you don't know how to make me weak in the knees, but for a relationship to work, it's got to be more than tingles that set you aflame. It's got to be about a personal relationship that can be counted on through thick and thin."

He dropped his hand from her neck and then twirled a strand of hair that was loose from her bun.

"I'm sorry for what was, and I know relationships need a foundation of mutual respect. I'm not trying to go around that, but I just want to make sure I can still give you those tingles."

She stepped back and gave him a curious look.

Bain laughed. "You didn't know that men can be insecure sometimes too. You are a beautiful woman, Clarrie. Maybe on top of everything else, I'm not to your liking anymore."

"Put that from your mind. To paraphrase, you've still got it."

Bain was about to reply when they were both interrupted by a woman clearing her throat.

"Excuse me. I hope I'm not interrupting."

Clarissa was grateful she had a hand anchored to Bain. The voice was attached to none other than her aunt Temperance Thorne.

<h1 style="text-align:center">Eight</h1>

"Clarissa, how unsurprising."

Clarissa tightened her grip on Bain and focused her attention on her aunt.

"Hello, Aunt."

Temperance Thorne walked into the room. She was a mousy looking woman. With brown hair pulled back into a bun and a rail-thin body that bordered on unhealthy, Clarissa had often wondered if her aunt was adopted. She was, at best, five foot three, and she had small eyes that missed nothing and criticized all.

Bain gripped her arm, breaking her concentration on her aunt, and gave her a smile.

"I'll leave you to this. If you need me, call me," he said for her ears alone. With that, he turned, nodded politely to Temperance, and then left.

As her aunt came in, she did a quick look around her office. It was a habit to make sure everything was in place before her aunt showed up. Anything that was out of place could become the basis for an argument. Clarissa had to say that she got her looks from her mother, but her aunt gave her the tenacity to plan for a goal.

When she was younger, her aunt would ask her what she wanted, and then she'd tell her to make a plan. While other children would receive random gifts for the holidays, Clarissa received what she had planned for. Her aunt told her it would help her to manage expectations in her life.

Old habits died hard. As her aunt approached, she wanted to sit down so as not to tower above her. She was self-conscious of the makeup on her face, and the blue dress that she had put on today now seemed inappropriate. Clarissa was mentally taking it all in, and she knew she would be found wanting.

Her aunt stopped on the other side of the desk with her black bag hanging over her forearm and her arms crossed in front of her chest.

"Haven't I earned a proper greeting?"

"Of course." Clarissa walked over and bent down to place a kiss on her cheek. She didn't embrace her because that was forbidden, but small shows of affection were mandated.

Clarissa stood up and gestured for her aunt to take a seat in the chair on the other side of the desk.

"I'm surprised to see you," she said.

"I'm sure you are. Was that Bain Parcel?"

"It was."

Temperance opened her bag and pulled out a newspaper clipping. She passed it to Clarissa. It was a picture of Bain. It was one of the many media pictures she had seen on the wall. It announced Bain was coming back to Sweet Blooms for the wedding of the season.

"I wonder why I need to find out about these types of things secondhand. I mean, I know I'm not in Sweet Blooms anymore, but you can't imagine how indisposed

I was when one of my bridge partners told me about this event instead of hearing it from you.”

“I don’t understand,” Clarissa said, pushing the article back towards her aunt.

“We can go over what this all means later. I’m staying at the hotel while I’m here. I don’t know what goes on at your place. Not that I’m asking. And I have to ask, is that your normal business attire?”

Clarissa stopped herself from looking down. She knew what she had on, and she wasn’t five anymore. “I can wear all sorts of dresses to work in.”

Her aunt took a little longer to scrutinize the dress before replying. “So it seems.”

Clarissa smiled. “I can see that this doesn’t meet with your approval, but I doubt anything in my closet would.”

Temperance’s jaw clenched, and she pulled her bag closer to her midriff. “I’m sure you can, Clarissa Ann.”

“It’s just Clarissa.”

“Excuse me?”

“My name is just Clarissa. No one uses my middle name.”

“Neither do I. Your name is Clarissa Ann Hastings. You don’t have a middle name.”

“Ann is listed on my birth certificate as my middle name. I would appreciate it if you could call me by my first.”

Clarissa folded her hands in her lap and looked at her aunt. This was the same old argument that they always had. They always ran into the same impasse. Clarissa knew her aunt wanted her to be grateful to a fault about her raising her, but she could never muster up enough worship for her. The last ten minutes had been a beast, and she couldn't even imagine how people did reunions.

"Well, I can see you are just as headstrong as ever," her aunt said.

Clarissa waited. If she denied she was headstrong, they'd argue. If she agreed they were headstrong, her aunt would go down the list of how to make her better and they'd wind up arguing. The best course of action was to change subjects.

"Auntie, I'm still a bit confused on why you're visiting now."

Her aunt sniffed. "I should think that would be obvious. I'm here to make sure you don't make yourself look silly by throwing yourself at Bain's feet and embarrassing the both of us."

"Okay, everyone, your mock dresses are in the dressing room. In the room are cards that tell you where to line up so we can do a mock walkthrough of the wedding," Annabelle, the wedding planner, yelled. "I'm timing this, so let's step lively and…go!"

Clarissa was sure this was going to be a catastrophe waiting to happen. This morning Bain had picked her up and told her there was going to be a mock rehearsal. The bride and groom party were doing it today. Due to the size of the wedding, it was being held in a hall in town. The hall was two stories, and if the truth was told, it was an old renovated mansion that had been saved as an integral part of history.

The wedding planner was dressed in fatigues and insisted a wedding would go right with practice, so the bride's and groom's parties were in rehearsal bootcamp. After the planner said go, Bain appeared next to Clarissa.

"I've been in the building and know where your room is."

"Isn't that convenient?"

Bain smiled at her. "It's so the couples will be right next to each other and can come down in pairs. Don't be so suspicious of me yet."

Clarissa sighed but followed him up the double set of fifteen steps to the second floor. By the time she got there, she was sure she should have worn flats. Bain paced himself but more than once, with a twinkle in his eye, he looked over his shoulder.

"You know I could carry you up the steps."

Clarissa smiled. "Or not. I have a rule: I may not be the first, but I won't be the last one up these steps."

When they made it to the rooms, Bain opened the door, and they both heard Annabelle from below. "We've got 40 minutes to make the couple happy, so let's move it!"

Clarissa went into the room saw a little card on the vanity with her name and was relieved she was in the right place. The room wasn't big. It was a dressing room with two doors. She saw the dress on the mannequin and quickly switched dresses.

The dress was a mermaid dress with a zipper in the back and three-quarter sleeves. Clarissa had no problem stepping into the dress. Putting her arms in the sleeves was a challenge, but it was the zipper that was her undoing. She looked around the for a hanger, hoping to pull the zipper up her back.

"Move along up there; it's been ten minutes already!" Annabelle called out.

Clarissa thought she saw a wire hanger, took three steps, and had to readjust her steps so she wouldn't fall. She barely grabbed the nearest wall.

"You have got to be kidding me!"

"Clarrie, let's go!"

Clarissa took a deep breath and took little steps to the door. When she whipped it open, Bain was there with a jacket.

"Is that your mock dress-up?"

"Yes, the guys voted jackets were enough. The bridal party needed as many fittings as possible. Get your card and—"

"You have to zip me up."

"What?"

Clarissa pulled him into the room. "Zip it up, hurry."

Bain grabbed the zipper, and it made it just to the small of her back.

"Clarrie, it's not going."

"I'm going to take a breath, and then you pull it."

"Clarrie—"

Clarissa turned around and faced him. "You wanted me in the party. I want to make a good impression."

Bain shrugged. Clarissa took a breath, and after three attempts, they got the zipper up to her shoulder blades. Clarissa heard little shuffling feet outside the door and knew the other women were leaving.

Frustration was a tangible beast in the room, and in a moment of frustration, Clarissa wiped the first errant tear.

"Clarrie, don't. It's not that bad. We can fix this."

"No, it's whatever. I'll try another time, and then I'll just put mine back on."

"Clarrie, I don't like to see you unhappy."

"Well, tootley-doo for you."

Clarissa turned her back to Bain and waited for another futile attempt. She would be the talk of the party, and she wasn't even trying. She was sure there was a logical reason, but she was hoping that today would be a good start for her.

"I've got an idea," Bain said.

Clarissa turned towards him, and he ripped the sleeves off of the dress and the faux lace that went all the way to her shoulder blades.

"Now the dress is fine. Grab your shoes."

Just like that, she grabbed her shoes and the card. That was seconds before Bain gave her a warning.

"Brace yourself." The next moment she was over Bain's shoulder, and for some inexplicable reason, she thought this was the funniest moment ever.

"Okay, Clarrie, open the note. Where are we going?"

She could barely hold her shoes and the note. "South entrance garden."

He ran down the steps, and as they went on, she could hear other members of the wedding party. When he pushed through the door, he set her on her feet, and they arrived just in time to hear Annabelle who was walking up and down the lane of pairs.

"I'm glad you all made it," Annabelle started. Then she looked at Clarissa and Bain and continued speaking. "Well, I'm glad most of you made it intact. That was nineteen minutes. It was entirely too slow. The south entrance is where you'll line up before the ceremony, so I need you to do this in fourteen minutes. We'll do it again."

Everyone groaned. Then, as if the heavens disagreed as well, a deluge of water fell from the sky. Clarissa kicked off her shoes and ran with Bain back to the house. By the time they got upstairs, they were still laughing about the whole affair.

Bain took her to his dressing room, and he had a chaise lounge in his.

"How come you get the lounge chair room?"

Bain shrugged. "You need an agent to see to these things for you."

Clarissa rolled her eyes. "Whatever."

A few moments later, Annabelle knocked on his door. Clarissa got up and stood behind the door while Bain answered it.

"Bain, have you seen Clarissa?"

"I'm sure she's around. What's up?"

"It looks like it will be doing this all day, so we're going to pick this back up tomorrow."

"I'll let her know."

"Do you need a lift anywhere since it's an early day?" Clarissa was behind the door, and she had to put her hand over her mouth.

"No, Annabelle, thanks."

"If you decide to change your mind…"

"I'll let you know. See you tomorrow."

Bain closed the door, and Clarissa walked with her hands on her hips and wiggled her eyebrows. She sashayed closer to him and puckered her lips a couple of times.

"Do you want to hook up since it's an early day, Bain?" she said in a mockingly sexy voice.

She could see the color rise and his face flushed from embarrassment. "Okay, you've had your fun."

"Did she ask for your number?" Clarissa had asked it as a joke, but when he didn't answer, she turned away and muttered to herself. "That must be so commonplace for you."

"Hey, it's not something I ever get used to, and since I'm with someone, it's a non-starter."

Clarissa turned so quickly she almost hit Bain as she stood up. "A non-starter? How long have you been with someone? Why are you—" She stumbled backward until she tripped over the shoes and fell back onto the chaise.

He went to her, kneeled down, and grabbed her hands. "Since I found out I'm still married, all numbers are non-starters," he said.

"Oh, I-I…"

"I know you blocked off the day to be here. Would you care to spend some time with me?"

Clarissa thought about telling him no and going back to the office, but he was right; she had the rest of the day off, and if truth be told, she didn't want to go back to her office because her aunt was bound to show up there sooner or later.

She gave him a wide smile. "You don't sound as smooth as Annabelle, but I'll go with you."

"Whew! I'm glad because I'm already on my knees."

Clarissa laughed. "Give me a moment to get dressed. Where are we going?"

"It's a surprise."

Clarissa was skeptical.

"If you don't like it, we'll leave, and I'll owe you one."

"With odds like that, Bain, give me five and we'll go."

"Then let me one-up them. You stay in your room until I knock to get you. I'll be right there."

Clarissa went to her room and put on her dress. It must have been five minutes later when he knocked. When she opened the door, he handed her a paper bag.

"What's this?"

"Look."

Clarissa brought the bag in and set it on the vanity. She pulled out a pair of her jeans and her favorite red top.

"I still have some of your clothes. They're in the house. I had them laundered, and I thought you'd be more comfy…"

Clarissa held the clothes to her chest and looked at Bain. The clothes brought back so many memories, and they hit her all at once. She wasn't sure she could trust herself to speak, and Bain made it easy not to.

"I'll give you a few," he said, and he backed out of the room.

Nine

Bain had taken a big chance of bringing her clothes. He needed to find his Clarrie, and the woman who strode through Sweet Blooms wasn't it. How does a man make up for doing the unforgivable? He didn't know if it was possible, but Clarrie was worth trying.

When the doors opened, she was dressed in blue jeans and a red shirt that had ruffles off the shoulder. Her hair was in a ponytail, and for a moment, he thought they were back in time before his pride had ruined everything.

"I hope you're not just going to stare at me for the day because I'm going to get bored real quick."

He smiled and held out his arm.

"Well, then, let me not keep you waiting."

When they went outside, she went to his car, and he called out to her.

"Come on, Clarrie, our ride is over here."

"We came in this car, Bain. I know it's hot, muggy, and it rained fiercely, but this is your car," she insisted. He walked up to her and tilted her head back to look into her eyes.

"Trust me, Clarrie. I won't let you down."

Then the bent down and placed a quick kiss on her lips. "I brought you clothes; give me a little more faith on the ride."

She nodded, and he took her hand. He hoped this worked. When he rounded the corner of the old house and heard her squeal with joy, he knew it had.

"Oh, my goodness, is that our truck?"

Bain nodded, and she ran towards it. The truck was the ugliest thing ever. It was a miracle that it ran at all, and it was the first thing the both of them had bought together. He watched her open the cab and turn the engine. Of course, it didn't turn on the first go, but on the second one, it did.

"Bain! Bain! Get in and let's go!"

He walked to the driver side and crooked his finger towards her.

"I love you, Clarrie, but I've been a victim of your driving before. So move over."

She leaned out the window and batted her lashes at him.

"Come on, Bain," she said as she blinked innocently.

"If you do that any harder, you'll take flight. Now move over, gorgeous!"

"I want you to know that while the truck is a plus, me not driving is a demerit for you. I hope whatever you have planned is amazing!"

Bain got in the truck and looked at her pouting in the seat next to him. "Me too."

As they pulled out, the skies opened up again, and they were encased in a world of water. Only the lights ahead could be seen in front of them.

"Bain, where are we going?"

"You'll know it when we get there, and we are almost there. It's ten minutes from here."

Clarissa laughed. "Bain, everything is ten minutes from where you are."

"See? I'm always telling the truth."

The rain subsided, and then they were at the ice cream parlor. It had changed hands a couple of times, but it was always there. When Bain came home, it was the first place they'd go.

"You want a cone with me?"

She looked at him, and again, she was speechless.

"You remembered."

"I've had nothing but time to remember what I lost. Will you have a cone with me?"

"Yes, I will." The smile on her face made all the chances worth it.

He ordered their cones and then went to find her sitting in their booth.

He placed the cones down. He had gotten one vanilla for him and strawberry with sprinkles for her.

They sat down and ate their cones, and the moment was just like it always was: perfect.

"I imagine you must have a favorite ice cream spot near you?"

"You'd imagine wrong. I haven't had any since you left."

She put her spoon down and looked at him.

"I don't get it, Bain. Who are you? How can it be you are so in love with me, yet it went so wrong?"

He took a deep breath and squared his shoulders.

"I was dumb. I had a football career, and I had you. Then I had an injury and the only thing they said I was good for was to take pictures of."

"Modeling has done good things for people."

"It's true, but I was ashamed. I went from tackling linemen to posing with women. I wasn't doing anything, and I didn't know how to deal with it. When you came and saw me with Natalya and left, I knew you were embarrassed as well, and then I ran. I was scared. I was dumb, and I messed up."

"Bain, don't—"

He interrupted her. "I thought a part of what you married was a football guy, not a model, and I ran so I didn't have to see you disappointed in me."

Clarissa reached out and caressed his cheek.

"I married Bain, the man. Not Bain the football guy or Bain the model, although I'm not complaining about the gorgeous fringe benefits. You look totally hot. But if you didn't, it wouldn't have mattered. You still make me laugh, and I would still love you."

"Then why are we at odds now?"

"Because it's not enough to just trust you. I need to know we both trust each other. Before I trusted you, but you didn't trust our love enough to tell me. Now, I don't know if I can trust you enough to give you my heart back."

They finished their ice cream cones and he picked up the napkins from the table.

"But you still love me, right?"

She leaned across the table and pulled his face to hers. She pressed butterfly kisses along the seam of his mouth, then she traced his eyebrows and brought her hands to his chin. She placed a quick kiss on his chin as well.

"Bain, I think the problem here is that sometimes love alone just isn't enough. It's time to go."

With that, she got up and walked out of the shop. He couldn't stand after that. It was a silent gut punch that he couldn't deflect or curl into. He couldn't tell anyone how he got up from the table or took her home.

When he got home, he sat on his couch, picked up the picture of Clarrie smiling that he kept in a frame, and let the silent tears run down his face. He looked at the frame that said *Love is eternal.*

Ten

Clarissa was looking out her window instead of working. Her thoughts were wandering as she thought about the outing she had with Bain. A smile curved her lips as she thought about the sprinkles.

"You've got a walk-in."

Clarissa turned around and looked at Jessica at the door with a wide smile on her face. "Who is it?" Clarissa was nervous; it had to be her aunt Temperance, and she braced herself for it.

"I think it's someone you'd like to see," Jessica said.

Clarissa looked beyond Jessica and saw Bain leaning against the door jamb. He waved at her over Jessica's head, and she had to contain herself. Jessica glanced behind her and looked up at Bain with stars in her eyes.

"I'll leave you two," she said sheepishly.

Bain came in and took a seat in front of her and leaned back. He moved as if every move was calculated to make a woman look at him. Working as a model kept him fit, but there was something about him that was just Bain. The just Bain quality made him eligible to star as a lead in a Disney film or be the model on the cover of a romantic novel. When he focused his attention on her, she felt as if she were the only woman in the world.

"Hi," he said as he looked at her. "How's your day going?"

She wanted to say, "Much better now that you're here," but she had to get a grip on life.

"It's the same old same old. People want money, licenses, and have ideas, but they don't know how to execute them. It's always a challenge to match planners with dreamers. You haven't seen my aunt lately?"

"I haven't found her lurking after me or contacting my agent."

"You're lucky. I'm sure she's saving it for me," Clarissa said.

"Why would she contact me?" Bain asked.

"I think she was insulted. I didn't tell her you were here. I never know what's going to come from that direction."

"Sounds like it's always a new adventure with her."

Clarissa thought on it, and a sour taste came to her mouth. "I think it's better because I'm older. It just makes me wonder why she's here. She left Sweet Blooms as soon as I moved out. For her to come back, there's got to be a reason."

She was talking to him as if he were a part of her life. Like he needed to know what she was thinking or doing. Bain made it so easy to talk. That was one of the reasons she'd fallen for him in the first place. Bain made it easy for her to be her. Was she falling into the same trap again? Was she…

"Ouch!"

Clarissa jumped up and went to Bain. He had his hands on both sides of his head.

"Bain, what's wrong?"

He pulled his hands down and looked into her concerned face. "You were thinking so hard it was hurting my head."

She went from concern to outrage in seconds. "Really, Bain? I thought something was wrong, but you're just kidding around."

Bain grabbed both of her hands and brought them to his lips.

"My love, forgive me, but you were really working yourself up thinking away. I'm here to help."

"How?" she asked as she tried to take her hands back.

"I think I'm causing you anxiety and you're overthinking everything when we are together or even around each other. We have to see each other entirely too much in meetings and outings for you to be worried. So I think we can minimize that by me giving you a heads up when it'll be a me and you moment."

She could see that he had really put some effort into this idea. It was sweet and misguided. As if knowing when an attack was going to happen made it easier.

"Okay, so you'll give me a heads up on what's going on? How long will these random moments of trying to get me back occur?"

Bain grinned. "I feel hurt. Is this your way of saying that these moments are too infrequent? You need more."

Clarissa cleared her throat and then looked at their joined hands. He opened up his hands, and she went back to the safety of the desk.

"I'm not asking for more. It's not just your time you're wasting; it's mine. I need to know how long to allow for these shenanigans."

"Well, that is the first time I've ever tried to win a woman's heart and she calls it shenanigans."

"Live and learn; at this rate, it won't be the last time."

"Did I tell you that one of the things I admire about you is your grit."

She sat back and looked at him long and hard. "Have you been reading one of those books on how to talk about feelings?"

Bain laughed. "No, but do you think I should? For you, I'd give it a shot."

Clarissa waved him off. "Enough, Romeo. I've had enough."

Bain stood up and bowed. "Well then, let me tell you that I'll see you in the morning to begin the wooing of my love."

"In the morning?"

"Yes, when the sun falls upon your house and lifts your soul to—"

"Stop! I get it, but you do know I'm off tomorrow."

"Love is never off, but yes, I do."

"Well, you better make it good."

"Until tomorrow, my fair shrew."

Clarissa laughed as he exited her office. He was impossible. One minute he was business Bain and then the next he was jokey Bain. He could be all of the seven dwarfs. This was going to wreck her life. Bain was still an unstoppable force to be reckoned with.

In the quiet of her office, as the world went on its way, she came to a conclusion. She couldn't do this with Bain. He was just too much Bain. She needed someone quieter, meeker, someone not so loud. Someone not so flamboyant. She'd take tonight and try to figure out a way to tell Bain this deal wasn't going to make it. The wedding was a go. The wooing was off.

Bain was more nervous going to Clarrie's door than he was going on an audition for a modeling gig. He knew she was wavering. At one point, he thought she might call the whole thing off. He was in the fight of his life with a losing hand.

That was one of the reasons he had stopped by the Sweet Blooms bakery and begged the older woman there for any hints on what Clarrie liked. He would have paid her three times the amount because she knew exactly what Clarrie ordered for herself. As a result, he had a box of six chocolate eclairs with vanilla pudding filling—not crème or whipped goodness but vanilla pudding.

She didn't know how close she'd come yesterday when she asked him if he had been reading books on his emotions. No, but he had been reading books on how to woo a woman after ending up in the dog house. While it was informative, none of it seemed to fit his Clarrie.

He could look past her amazing figure and fitted clothing to see the real her. As he went through the town, he realized, when he heard random comments on how she was removed from the town and thought she was too good for them, how well she hid herself. If only they knew, he was the problem. It was him that made her retreat into herself. He was sure she did it as a protective measure at first, and now it was just second nature. They didn't know the woman who preferred jeans and peasant tops.

He was about to knock on the door when it opened.

"How long were you going to stand out here?"

"I was trying to think of one of those sexy lines women love that make history."

She leaned against the door and gave him a smirk. "Like?"

"Like you complete me."

She laughed and took a step back. He let out a breath and kept his gifts under his arms.

"You brought…?"

"I bear gifts of coffee and eclairs."

"Smart man. Come into the kitchen so we can talk."

"Uh-huh. Every man knows nothing good comes from a woman who says let's talk."

She got two cups and then sat down. He opened the box and placed a napkin and an éclair in front of her.

"Maybe I should have waited until I told you the news?"

"It doesn't matter; we'll get through it no matter what," he said.

"I think we should do the wedding but the whole us thing we should nix," she said.

"Wow, I think I need an éclair after that statement."

"Bain, this isn't a joking matter."

"I'm not joking. What's wrong?"

"It's you, Bain."

He took a bite of the éclair and tried to collect his thoughts. The sense of panic running through him was so intense he had to tap his foot against the kitchen table to release some of the energy. He swallowed the éclair and pushed it down his throat then faced the only woman he'd ever love.

He could see she was distressed, and again, he was

the cause. "Am I that far gone, Clarrie? If you say it, I'll believe it."

She reached out and covered his hand. "Bain, no."

"Then what is it? What do you want me to do? I know I have a whole lot to get by, but I'm looking for a chance, even though I don't deserve one."

"Bain, you are impressive all the time, and I don't think I can make any good decisions around you. I want a normal looking guy. With a normal career and—"

"Clarrie, you know me. I've got the same problems as any other guy!"

She sat back and folded her hands over her chest. "Now really, Bain, that was a bit too much."

"Is that it? You think I'm not normal?"

"I don't see it, Bain."

He took a breath and relaxed. This he could fix.

"I think this goes both ways, actually."

"What?"

Bain shook his head. "I've been in town, and according to them, you wake up perfect. You never sweat, and you go to sleep in an amniotic chamber to be forever youthful."

She stopped, looked at him, and then covered her mouth as she laughed.

"Come on! Me?"

Bain shrugged. "I'm just saying we should both have to prove our normalness."

"Okay, I'll take that dare. Let's go."

"Ladies first."

"Okay, I use mayonnaise and beer in my hair to condition it," she said with a smile.

"I use coffee grounds and leave-in conditioner to kill those red highlights in my hair," he replied.

"No way! You have to have a stylist."

"I'm a man. No other man is going to do my hair except a barber, and no woman is going to color my hair. Have you seen what colors women come out with from the beauty salon? Nope. It worked for my dad, and it'll work for me. Coffee grounds."

"Okay, I wear a shaper to give me my figure. It's not what they think it is."

"No way!"

She waved him off as she laughed. "Don't even."

"That's got to be the number one woman trick on a guy," he said, laughing.

"Okay, come on, Mr. Normal, what you got!"

"I use lotion on my body every time I get out of the shower. It helps to keep my skin moisturized, so I don't need as much sunscreen."

"What? You mean when you took all that time in the bathroom, you made me think it was your hair, but you were—"

"Lathering up. If I don't, the skin will go south quick."

Her eyes widened. "You worry about your skin?"

"I had acne when I was younger, so having peeling skin when I'm an adult is a no go. And, by the way, I have sensitive skin. So all of the products I buy are hypoallergenic."

Once the both of them had finished laughing at their normalness, she looked at him and whispered, "This is scarier than I thought it would be."

"Ditto."

"My aunt always taught me that I get what I plan for, and with you, I didn't plan with you, and you left. I want to try again, but there isn't a plan to trust and love someone. That makes this really risky."

He covered her hand and squeezed it. "We are worth this risk. I'm older, wiser, and better."

She laughed. "Okay, let's not overdo it. I'll give you older."

"Ow, the woman wounds me, but I'll take all of these assaults for love."

"The eclairs were perfect, thank you."

"Well, enjoy them. I think we should go for a walk afterward."

She eyed him. "Are you trying to say something?"

He stood up and grinned. "I'm trying to say we are going on a walk shaper free so you can concentrate."

"Concentrate on what?"

"Working out, of course. It's a part of my life, and I want to share it with you."

He saw her giving it some thought. He wanted her to remember it wasn't just his life. She was the one who had taught him to find a horse to ride or go on a run, but either one would clear the head. It was as if he could see the light go on inside her head.

"Okay, let me get my running gear, and I'll meet you in the front. I hope you remember how to run," she teased.

When she went back inside the house, he wanted to yell, "Yeah!" It wasn't big, but he was making progress. He just needed time.

Eleven

Clarissa got out of her car and looked at the house that dominated the Cade Ranch. She'd been here before for the opening of the on-site workshop, and for other official business, but today she was here as a guest.

"Talk about a lifestyle," she muttered to herself. The house was beautiful, and the grounds as well. When she walked up to the door, a woman with a butler smiled at her.

"Please walk around the house; you'll see the bridal party is there."

So if Clarissa understood this correctly, they were meeting today to get the measurements again so maybe next time she could do the rehearsal in a dress that fit. She'd hadn't known what to expect, but Daisy had told her to think big and comfy. As she came around the corner, it became clear. A woman greeted her and took her shoes and provided slippers. As she walked the path, another person offered her a drink of iced tea or lemonade. The last person took her measurements and then told her to continue walking.

"Clarissa?"

She had to take a second look because it appeared to be Hannah, but she was in a white robe. Behind her was a smiling Daisy, also in a robe.

"Did I come overdressed, or was there a theme?" she asked, pointing at them.

"No, you didn't miss a thing. All of our clothes were being taken by the seamstress who is doing the final measurements, and we have a masseuse on hand to destress.

Clarissa gave them one more look and then followed the women into a large tent that was set up outside.

Clarissa had gotten a delivery and a personal message reminding her she was a part of the party, and she needed to be fitted. She followed Hannah and Daisy into the large tent. All around there were chaise lounges and pillows on the floor. To the far left were two massage tables, and members of the bridal party were on them getting a massage.

"I know it takes a bit to get used to," Hannah said, taking a seat at one of the round tables. As soon as they sat, several waiters came with several types of drink. "As you can see, Adam has gone overboard."

Clarissa took another lemonade and looked around. She knew she didn't want this from Bain. She wanted his attention and love, but this was a bit over the top.

"Are you comfortable with the wedding program? I know Bain said he would go over it with you, but I wanted to make sure," Hannah asked.

"We did, so I'm good, and thank you for including us." Clarissa felt as if she were a fish out of water. She knew these women but didn't seem to really know them.

Daisy interrupted her thoughts.

"I thought with everything you and Bain are going through, it would be good for you to get your fitting and have someone to talk to."

Clarissa looked around the tent and wondered what either of these women would know about trusting a man. The burning feeling was coming back, and she tried to blink it away.

Daisy reached out and touched her hand.

"You can tell us. We're here to help."

Girlfriends. That wasn't something she had experienced before. When she was in school, girls hung out with her because guys did. It was about trying new things and trusting people.

"Well, to be honest, Bain and I are trying, but we'll see. I don't know what we'll do, but our time is coming to a close, and I don't feel any closer to making up my mind than I was before."

She didn't know what to expect, and she looked away, expecting everyone to ignore it and go on with their conversations. She was frustrated and torn, and if she were honest, she really wanted to go home and cry.

"Is the problem love or trust?" Hannah asked.

Clarissa's head popped up. Why did she give those two options?

"Is there something he said or that you can see when we're together?" Clarissa asked in a small voice.

"No."

"Then why those two options?"

Hannah smiled sadly. "At the end of the day, most relationships come down to one of those two things."

Daisy nodded as she sipped her lemonade. "Mine was trust. It was hard to trust Patrick, and he already had an alternative agenda when he came."

Clarissa remembered Patrick arriving and how he had tried to get her to buy the land from him. More than one person thought it was a bit too convenient when Patrick decided that he had feelings for Daisy.

"But you got past it, right?" Clarissa asked hopefully.

"Eventually, yes, but it wasn't overnight, and I have to tell you that every so often I still have a lingering doubt about if he settled for me to get the land."

"And how do you handle it?"

Daisy smiled. "We talk about it, and then we work on why I feel that way and how to help me."

Clarissa looked at Hannah, who nodded.

"And the same thing happened to you?"

Hannah looked at her and Daisy and then sighed. "No, the problem was love. It was odd. Trust was easy for me because it's so black and white, but when you have a child, love is an important intangible that you need, but no one can really prove. So Adam spent a lot of time finding my heart and wooing it before I conceded that he did love me. It was at a point I almost lost him before I did."

"Bain is a star," Clarissa said. "He's got this high profile job, and he's going to have groupies, and his life will be filled with different women who are beautiful and—"

Hannah reached out and touched Clarissa's hand.

"Are we talking about trust or are you worried that he'll stray and you won't be enough?"

Clarissa heard the words, and they felt like a stone in her stomach.

Would she be enough? Was she really that insecure? Was she scared of a little competition?

She looked at the women around her, and a smile broke out across her face.

"I can see the merit of this girl thing. You all are right. I don't need to be insecure; he came all this way for me, so I'm looking for ghosts that don't exist."

She took another healthy sip of her lemonade and straightened her back.

Daisy cleared her throat, and Clarissa looked up.

"So, since we are all sharing and all, I have to say I've always wanted to ask you some questions," she said shyly.

"Go for it."

"Where do you buy your clothes, and how do you find time to work out? You always look great."

Clarissa laughed. "Ladies, let me introduce you to body shapers and my favorite online magazine."

"So what is the occasion that prompted you to see me tonight?" Clarissa asked as Bain laid out a blanket in the back of the bed of the pickup truck.

"Well, I'm going to go on a trip for a few days, and I'll be back. I just need to settle some shoots, and then I'll be home."

"I like the sound of that. I'll be waiting here, and we can do ice cream scoops when you get back," Clarissa said as she laughed.

Bain had pulled up in their truck and drove out to Star Point. He hadn't said what this was about, but he had said he would be by late and here they were.

Clarissa was feeling odd. First, Star Point had another name, and it was a place that the kids went to find some privacy from prying eyes. She loved him. She wanted to work on their relationship, but she didn't think she was ready to move beyond that point.

Now she was nervous and didn't want to disappoint, but she knew her boundaries. He had brought some pillows and placed them in the back. Although she knew they were outside, it was still cozy and private. When he was done making the bedding and fluffing the pillows, he held out his hand.

"Bain?"

"I'm asking you to lay down with me and dream."

She looked at him as if he were a little off.

"Is that what we're calling it these days?"

Bain laughed. "Clarrie, really?"

She raised her eyebrow at him.

"I mean it. If you think I'm being inappropriate, you will get the first blow."

She took his hand and got on the truck bed and laid down. He lay next to her, and they both looked up at the night sky. They lay there for a few moments before Clarissa broke the silence with a question.

"Not that I'm not comfy, because I am, but what are we doing?"

"I'm working up the courage to talk to you about my dreams."

Clarissa turned her head toward Bain, but he was looking straight ahead.

"How about I help by asking questions?"

She heard him sigh and then nod in the affirmative.

"I dream about a large house that has lots of bedrooms so I can have kids. All of the kids don't have to be mine. Maybe some of them are foster kids, and I can give them a home that they could only dream about."

"Huh, well, I was thinking about a fixer-upper."

"What?"

Bain looked at her and nodded. "Yeah, I was thinking a fixer-upper would be great. With each finished room, I'd get a kid."

"What, you think kids come as rewards for rooms being built?" she scoffed.

"No, but I'm thinking it's something to work for."

"Okay, let's stop with the house. Let's agree if we get a house, it's in good condition, and you can add on to it."

"Agreed!"

"Okay, we need a dog. I think dogs are important pets." Clarissa looked at Bain, and he agreed.

"Whew! I was a little worried. Well, I think a Great Dane or maybe a Shepherd."

When he didn't agree right away, she looked at him. He continued to stare into the sky.

"Bain?"

"Well, I was thinking we would get something small."

"Small?"

He looked at her sheepishly. "I thought it would be better to have the dog always stay with the kids. Little dogs make a lot of noise, and they can sleep in the kid's room."

Clarissa looked at him with new eyes. He turned and saw her staring.

"Were we really married? I feel like I didn't know things about you that I would have told someone that I knew for sure."

He turned on his side and smiled at her. "That's what this is all about, right? It's about you getting to know me and me getting to know you. This is our new beginning. If you want it?"

Clarissa smiled.

"I do. I'm willing to give us a chance. I love you, and I trust you," Clarissa said.

Bain smiled and leaned down. The anticipation of the kiss was part of it all. As his shadow fell across her face, she closed her eyes and let the warm sensation bloom from her stomach until it wrapped around her. Sensations flooded her body and coalesced just where their lips met. Just when she thought he was about to deepen the kiss, he pulled back.

When he sat up and began to scoot off the truck, she sat up and pushed up to see him.

"Bain?"

"Clarrie, it is time to go."

"Bain?"

"No, Clarrie, it's time to go."

"I thought—"

He stopped and looked at her. "Clarrie, we've already been married, so I know what I'm walking away from, and that's why I'm packing up now."

She smiled. "Bain?"

He stopped and looked at her. "Yeah?"

"Thanks."

They packed up, and he took her home. She stood at the door as he left.

"Come back soon and think of me."

"You'll be my only thought, Clarrie."

Like a schoolgirl, she went to bed with her hand on her lips, remembering his kiss and his promise in her ears. Yes, she had made the right decision to give her and Bain a chance.

Twelve

She must have been tired when she thought she could trust Bain.

"Agnes has been kind enough to do the diligent and hardworking job of collecting articles that mention Sweet Blooms and what we are doing lately," the mayor said.

"It's more like she's reading all that trash anyway and she can finally do something worthwhile with it," Jerry said from the other side of the table.

Clarissa tried not to laugh as the two older members of the board engaged in their usual banter.

"Jerry, if you only knew how hard it was for me. I have to switch out glasses when I go through all of the articles, and some of them are just so outrageous that it doesn't even make sense."

Jerry grunted. "You see, she was already doing it. I mean, I'm glad someone does, but let's not make her out to be the next best thing since white bread."

Agnes sat up and folded her arms under her chest. "Jerry, you make me sound like some gossipmonger, but I'm telling you that if I didn't do this, who would look out for our good name and make sure we are being perceived the right way?"

"Now, now, let's look at what Agnes has found." The mayor handed out a folder with some newspaper clippings. "My thought is, we want to use the publicity and put these items on our websites and our news-papers."

Everyone opened the folder and looked inside.

Clarissa flipped through the pictures that said that Sweet Blooms was getting a power boost from the rich and famous. Then she ran into a small article that showed Bain with Natalya. The article read: *Is the world's most perfect couple going to Sweet Blooms and making it a power headquarters?* As Clarissa read through the article, it spoke about how the couple had been seen at dinner and how the rumors were already in the wind that perhaps Cade's wedding could be a double one.

Clarissa looked up and found Agnes looking at her. Then everyone went round-robin suggesting what the town could use in other venues. She'd spent too many years having people stare at her, waiting for a reaction that she wasn't going to give them the benefit of.

"I think the flower power terms they have are great, and maybe we can put some more flower motifs on our websites," she began. "It will also give us a chance to showcase Sweet Blooms Café.

"I think we should think about inviting the model Natalya. You're part of the wedding party, Clarissa. Do you have any insights if it's true what they say about Natalya and Bain?"

"We don't know what the rich and famous do, Agnes; they have their own set of rules. I don't know if we want to invite that to Sweet Blooms," the mayor concurred.

Clarissa couldn't stop the conversation. She was so

angry and doing her best not to explode. How could he? Did he just leave her and go to Natalya? She was internally counting, knowing there was a good reason for it all. She just had to wait, and he'd explain. If she didn't kill him first.

"I think star power is good. Bain has been to the town. Maybe we should ask him if he'll offer himself as a date," Agnes suggested.

"The way your old mind is working, you'd have the man half-naked in the street," grumbled Jerry.

"Really, everyone. I know that Bain is a celebrity, but we need to have respect for his person," defended Clarissa. Of course, when he came home, she was going to run him through the wringer.

Agnes sniffed. "He's used to being shown off. I'm not asking him to do anything that he doesn't already do."

Then, amidst Clarissa being mad at Bain, she heard the prejudice that Bain was afraid of. She had heard him say that he was ashamed of being a model, but she couldn't understand why. With Agnes's words about how she didn't even think he was really working because he was a model let her know that his fear wasn't unfounded and she hadn't really understood.

The mayor looked as if she were reluctantly agreeing. "Well, Clarissa, we do have to think that he's been modeling for a while. I'm sure he's a nice person, but at the end of the day, he takes pictures all day. We can use the publicity for a couple of those pictures. It shouldn't be a big thing for him. After all, they're pictures."

Clarissa put her sense of betrayal and her agenda to do all sorts of things to Bain to the side. Her aunt Temperance had taught her this: if nothing else, you handle house business at home, not in public.

"I can't believe you all are dismissing him and his efforts because you believe that what he does is so simple."

"With such a fickle career, he's not like the rest of us," Agnes chimed in.

With her anger cooling her tones and Agnes giving her a target for the turmoil she was feeling inside, Clarissa addressed her right away.

"I wonder, Agnes, have you talked to him, by chance?"

Agnes shifted in her seat. "No."

"Maybe you know the family and his mother or grandmother told you something about him that they knew?"

"No"

"Well, certainly you're in the wedding party, and you have spent time with others who've spent time with him to come to these conclusions?"

"No, I haven't, but I don't have to see the wolf eat the sheep to know that he will."

"Then I hope you don't run into a dog that looks like a wolf and shoot him accidentally. What I'm saying to everyone is that modeling is hard; otherwise, we'd all do it. Two, we need to ask him what he'd like to do for us. I don't think we can just make assumptions about what he can do and how. The last one is one I didn't think I would have to say, but I'm going to. We have to give him a chance like anyone else in town. I'd hate to think that this new publicity we have has turned us into judgmental people."

Clarissa stared around the table; some people looked at the folder, and some peeped at the mayor. Clarissa could tell that she wasn't happy, but this was important. It was for Bain.

"Clarissa has a point. Let's look at what other options we can use in our publicity sites."

"I can't even tell you which one of these things is making me angrier," Clarissa said as she had lunch with Hannah and Daisy. "First, Agnes with the picture that shows that Mr. Trust Me, I Love You is hanging out with his old flame, and then Agnes suggesting that Bain is somehow not as hardworking as the rest of us because of what he does."

Daisy nodded and looked on with sympathy in her face, and she tossed another popcorn shrimp in her mouth.

"Daisy, if you keep popping a shrimp on every point she makes, you won't have enough shrimp," Hannah said.

Clarissa looked at the two women who had become her new friends. "Why did the both of you order an appetizer?"

Hannah sighed. "Because even with a shaper, if I ate like you do, Clarissa, I'd never fit into my dress."

Clarissa took a breath and let it out. "Am I making sense at least?"

"Completely!" said Daisy. "You were coming to the defense of your true love," she said.

"That's right. I was coming to the defense of the untrustworthy one," moaned Clarissa.

"You don't know yet," Hannah cautioned. "I can tell you it's a whole different animal being with a person who had a public life. Since I've been with Adam, I've seen things in the paper that claim everything from Adam having another family stashed away to he's really an alien and we've all been duped."

Clarissa stopped and then looked at the women at the table before they all broke out into laughter.

"What I'm saying is, give him a chance to explain," Hannah said. "Also, you'll have to not rise to the bait when other people come to push your buttons."

Daisy looked at her watch and had to excuse herself, leaving Hannah and Clarissa alone for lunch.

Hannah tapped the table to get Clarissa's attention.

"I know you and Bain are working on things, but I want you to think about today."

Clarissa sighed. "I don't think I was wrong—"

Hannah interrupted her. "I don't think you were wrong, either. I'm not saying that. What I am saying is this is a part of Bain's world. People will say things about him one way or another, and you're going to have to deal with that. You can't fight them all, and in truth, I don't answer two-thirds of them."

"But you know the rumors and the newspaper articles aren't true."

Hannah smiled and ate a shrimp. "You mean that I trust Adam and I don't worry about what those articles say? You would be right. I thought we had addressed the issue of trust between you and Bain."

Clarissa looked into her water glass and nodded.

"I thought so too."

"Well, I have to go, but I just want to prepare you for the day after tomorrow. We have a bride and groom party event set up by Annabelle. I know Bain said he would be coming back that morning."

"Fine. We'll do the event and then talk."

Hannah patted her hand. "Remember, this whole relationship thing is a work in progress."

Thirteen

Temperance knocked on the front door. She didn't bother to use the doorbell because she didn't want Clarissa to have an excuse for why she didn't hear her. She had contacted Clarissa three times already, and each time she had come up with some flimsy excuse about why she couldn't meet. Coming to her place was the most expedient way to get this meeting done.

She had been in town, and already she had gathered more than her fair share about the life Clarissa had been living. Temperance wasn't surprised. No matter how much she would have wished it otherwise, Clarissa was her mother's daughter.

She counted to ten and then she began to knock on the door again. If Clarissa didn't answer this time, she'd go around the back of the house and knock there.

"What is the emergency!" Clarissa said as she yanked the door open. When she saw who was at the door, Clarissa let out a sigh. "I was in the kitchen cleaning."

"Perhaps? Or maybe you were just hoping I'd go away."

Clarissa didn't deny it. Her only response was to compose her facial features and motion for Temperance to come in.

"Hello, Aunt."

"Thank goodness you remembered the most basic of manners."

Clarissa closed the door and then invited her to the sofa.

Temperance sat down and give the cushion a little bounce.

"The couch is a bit worn. You could probably get a better one if you didn't buy such a variety of dresses." When Clarissa didn't respond, she sat back until she was leaning against the pillows. "The pattern is a little too dark as well for this room. Are you getting it redone?"

Clarissa sat back in the high back chair and crossed her legs.

"I understand we don't share the same taste. Is that why you came by, to educate me on what is wrong with my personal sense of style?"

"No, there's no need for me to tell you what you already know is true." Temperance looked around and tried to find something that she could say positively about the place or about Clarissa, but nothing came to mind.

Looking at Clarissa sitting in the chair was like looking at her mother. Temperance never understood or had the confidence of her younger sister. Temperance was always the daughter that no one understood and who didn't shine. She would do the right thing and the safe thing. Her younger sister, of course, shined. She was the pretty one. She was the adventurous one. She had the fairytale wedding and the equally romantic death.

Everyone had adored her sister so much that when

she had died, they didn't even question if Temperance would take in her child. Obviously, nothing Temperance was doing was so important that she couldn't stop and take care of Clarissa Ann.

"I'm still not clear why you are here, Aunt Temperance," Clarissa asked.

"I came here to make sure you didn't disgrace yourself while Bain was here."

Clarissa stared at her and then laughed. "Oh, I'm so, so sorry. I know this is coming out wrong, but I think you just said you came here to help me preserve my reputation."

"I remember what it's like to be in Sweet Blooms, where people have a vision of what you should do regardless of what you wanted. I wanted to come here to help you with that, not to be laughed at."

"I'm sorry, really, I'm sorry. Would you like some tea or lemonade?"

"Lemonade sounds pleasant," Temperance said.

Clarissa came back with two glasses and set them on the coffee table between them.

"Please forgive my outburst; this day has been very trying. Maybe if we talk things out, I can get a clearer picture of what it is you're hoping to accomplish."

Temperance took a sip of the lemonade and nodded. The lemonade was too sweet, and she was about to say so when she saw Clarissa sitting on the edge of her seat, waiting.

"Thank you for the lemonade. It's different," she said.

The both of them sipped at their glasses for a few empty minutes before Temperance decided it was time to explain.

"You asked me why I came."

"Yes."

"The reason I'm here is because Bain came to town. I know there are a lot of people who will probably think you should go back to him. Of course, that would be tragic because of how it ended the last time, but public pressure can be harsh."

Clarissa placed her glass down on the table and nodded.

"It's good of you to be so concerned that you came out to tell me. I wish I had known you were coming, but I made plans to meet with some business owners for dinner."

"Of course, I want you to maintain your decency in town." She put the glass on the coffee table, which was definitely too low. Perhaps Clarissa didn't know how to decorate, or maybe there was another answer.

"Did this furniture come with this house? That would explain the oddities with the furniture."

Clarissa cut her off. "No, I picked every piece of furniture here."

"Oh, well, if you need some assistance with it to make it more female and cohesive…" As she stood up next to Clarissa, she could see how stiff Clarissa was standing. She realized that the helpful comments were being misinterpreted.

"Please, Clarissa, I had hoped you had grown out of that oversensitive nature of yours. I'm only mentioning things you should address so someone else doesn't see it, and then you find you are the object of town gossip the next day."

"I'm sure you meant your comments the way you always do."

Temperance could see this conversation was going poorly, although she was at a loss as to why. Just when she was about to say something, Clarissa interjected.

"I'm sorry we don't have more time. Maybe we can schedule for later on in the week?"

Temperance watched as Clarissa went to the door and opened it. She wasn't throwing her out exactly.

"Of course." She left the house and went to her car. She didn't have to turn to know that Clarissa wasn't at the door. There was never anyone at the door. Why would her niece be any different?

After last night, Clarissa was ready for Bain when he arrived with the groomsmen. Annabelle waited until they were all gathered at the dining room table before she explained the writing of the vows.

Annabelle was dressed in a floral dress, and she was all smiles today with her hair down.

"As a wedding planner, this is one of my favorite parts of the ceremony. It's when the vows are made. Some people use the traditional ones and let the priest recite the vows, and some couples ad-lib it. The couple has decided that each pair will say a vow as they walk in and then go to their respective sides. It's different, and I think I like it, so today we will work on what that wording will be.

"The bride and groom suggest you think about what vow you'd like to say. Think about them and what you'd wish for them."

The room was all aflutter, but Clarissa looked at Bain and wanted to strangle him. She was trying to get herself in the game. She wasn't going to think about her aunt wanting to save her from throwing herself at Bain, and she wouldn't think about Bain and his silly words on trust and then him high tailing it out to see Natalya.

After the announcement, Annabelle told each couple in the next room there was a small table with index cards where they could brainstorm and present when they were ready, hopefully within the next two days.

"Clarrie, I think this is such a great way to make vows."

"Yes, vows are important. They are like promises and other things that build trust."

"You're right." Clarissa watched Bain pick up the index card and a pen. "What do you think is important and represents Hannah and Adam?"

"I think couples should tell the truth."

"Honesty is a good one. Maybe something like, 'May you always be best friends as well as lovers?'"

Clarissa stopped and looked at him. He was smiling, and she couldn't see one sign that he'd just come from another woman.

"Clarrie, what's wrong?"

Clarissa looked around the room and realized this wasn't the place. "Can I talk to you outside for a minute?"

Bain and Clarissa walked to the front of the hall, smiling to all as they passed.

"What happened over the last couple of days, Bain?"

"I did some modeling jobs."

"I was in the committee meeting, and Agnes brought up a clipping of you and Natalya out with each other. There was even speculation in the article that you and her were going to get married."

He rolled his hand forward, indicating for her to keep going.

"And—"

"And?"

"Yes, Clarrie, and what is the question?"

"I thought you were going to work, and instead, you are having dinner with Natalya."

"Natalya and I work in the same industry."

"So you did go to see her?"

"Clarrie, you are mixing this up. I do a lot of shots with Natalya. It doesn't mean anything."

"Why didn't you tell me you were going to see her?"

"I told you I was going to work."

"She's the same woman I saw you with when we broke up. Don't you think that's important?"

Bain paced and ran his hands through his hair.

"Actually Clarrie, I don't think it's important. Do you want to know what my agent told me after I did the shoot? That I should call you. To give you a heads up about what might come out.

You know what I told him? I told him I didn't need to because you wouldn't believe the rubbish anyway."

"Bain, I'm saying you didn't tell me."

"And is that the way it would be every time I went to do a shoot? I can't do the shoot unless I tell you who I'm doing it with?"

Clarissa listened to Bain, and all of a sudden, the thing that seemed as though he was unreasonable and noncommunicative now seemed silly.

She reached out to touch his shoulder, and he took a step back.

"Bain, I'm sorry. I overreacted to nothing."

Bain looked at Clarissa.

"I don't know what happened here. What I do know is you said you'd trust me."

"I do trust you."

"Then why were you mad before you had even talked to me?"

Clarissa didn't say a thing; she just shrugged.

"I don't know."

Bain nodded. "Well, I don't know either. What I do know is if I decide to keep modeling, you're going to have to trust that I'm not hooking up with someone else or doing anything wrong. And even if you do think I am, I'd hope you'd at least ask me before you convict me one way or another."

"Bain."

"Give them my apologies. I need to unpack."

"Bain—"

Clarissa watched Bain walk away, and she didn't try to stop him because he was right.

Fourteen

"How can I love someone who makes me so crazy?" Bain moaned as he passed the lo mein to his agent, Roger. "She didn't even ask me; she just assumed that I was wrong. How am I going to be able to manage that if I decide to keep modeling?"

Roger looked at the greasy noodles and nodded along with Bain. They had decided to meet in the media trailer to have a pow-wow about what he was doing in his career. Roger wouldn't have cared if he had wanted to meet in the street in a bad alley. Bain was a moneymaker and a friend.

"Personally, I think the whole love thing is crazy, and I have no idea why people strive for it. It has tons of negatives."

Bain laughed at him and shook his head.

"Roger, really? You've never been in love?"

Roger waved his chopsticks around as he spoke.

"Once upon a time, I thought I was in love, and I left the relationship with half my income, the dog, and half of my dreams. No thanks, I'm good."

"One day, my friend, you'll get smitten by the right woman, and then you'll be with the rest of us."

"We're friends as well as business partners; don't wish bad luck on me."

Bain sat back and sighed. "You know the problem is that I love her. I messed up, it's true, but I thought we were good. This is one of those times where I feel like I'm stuck between a rock and a hard place."

Roger held up his hand.

"Okay, let me be the voice of reason here. It wasn't that long ago you were saying you weren't going to do modeling anymore. What changed?"

Bain put his carton to the side and looked at the media wall.

"I need to do something while I figure out what I want to do. I realize that I may not stay in the game long, that's true, but for me to go from traveling every couple of days to just sitting by and doing nothing, that's a bit extreme."

"Okay, I'll take that. That's a good reason, but not as good as you making so much money right now. I can't think why you wouldn't ride this out to the end, being that a model's lifetime in the business is relatively quick."

Bain laughed at Roger.

"You are always thinking about the dollar."

"It's an occupational hazard when you realize that the only thing you can do is market other people with talent. Okay enough about me, so we now understand why the change in stance on working or not. As your agent, and as your friend, I hope you've had these discussions about your work plans with her as well."

Bain looked away.

"Okay, see, this is another reason I'm not doing the love thing; all common sense just goes out the window.

Well, if the two of you manage to start talking to each other again, mention it."

"Second, you do realize that this is about trust and she's probably just insecure that you'll leave her again."

"I know, but what can I do? I feel like it comes down to she's either going to believe me or not," Bain complained.

"Reason number nine million why this love thing isn't for me is because it's not logical. You made a mistake, and she needs to forgive you. If she says she does, her head may agree, but her feelings haven't caught up."

"What am I going to do, Roger?"

"Well, although it's against my bottom line common sense, I think you should go talk to her. Women are big into the communication thing."

Bain had a plan. He was going to speak to Clarissa and set some ground rules and find out if they had something worth fighting for. It was a great plan. He stopped by the media trailer to drop off some paperwork for Roger when the door slammed open.

"Hello!"

Bain turned around at the familiar voice.

"Natalya?"

The petite woman with dark hair and signature cat eyes came into the trailer with her arms wide open. "Bain! I'm here, and I need your help."

Bain looked at Natalya and just stared. This couldn't be happening, could it? Just when he was sure he had a plan, now this.

"Natalya, how can I help you, and when can you leave?"

Natalya laughed and took a seat.

"I knew I could count on you, and I'm sure that this is all a mistake that we can fix in no time."

Bain sat down and put his head in his hands and let out a breath. This just couldn't be happening to him.

"We've got company," Natalya said.

Bain looked up and saw Roger standing in the door.

"Wow, Bain, you have the worst luck ever," he said as he laughed.

"Roger!" Natalya scolded.

"You'll forgive me if I don't join in with your festivities." Bain moaned.

"Yeah, I can see how you might view this as a negative situation. This is just a life lesson to me about the perils of love. But don't worry, I am sure that if anyone can get out of this, it would be you, Bain." Roger said skeptically.

Bain wished he had the confidence that Roger seemed to have in him about the situation. Knowing he had to talk to Clarrie had been a decision-maker, but this new event of Natalya showing up was a serious problem.

Roger looked at Natalya. "So what brings you to Sweet Blooms?"

"My agent has just blocked me from all of my money. I have the lawyers and other things working on it, but I need to work, so I came to cash in on a favor that I once extended to Bain," she said with a smile. "I wanted to shadow him on his assignments, so I can make sure I stay in the game. You know, until all of this blows over."

Natalya turned to Bain and shrugged. "It will be nothing. You won't even know that I'm here." She walked up to him and hugged him. "I know this is unexpected, and I know how you don't like to have your work life and your personal life mix. I get that, and I promise this won't be an inconvenience at all."

"I'm sure this will be like everything else, Natalya— a disaster waiting to happen."

Roger tilted his head to the side. "Listen, go and take care of your business. I'll do what I can for Natalya."

"Thank you," Bain said. "I appreciate the help. I'm going to be spending the afternoon out, but I'll be back after that. Get Natalya settled in the hotel for me?"

Roger nodded, and Bain left. He was hoping to do a breakfast meeting with Clarrie, but that wasn't an option. Now he needed to see if he could catch Clarrie for lunch. Just as he was going out the door, his cell rang.

"Hello?"

"Bain?"

"Clarrie, I was just thinking about you."

"I'm glad. I wanted to talk to you. Do you have time for a late breakfast?"

"Sure!"

"Come by my place, and we'll eat."

"I'm on my way."

Bain hung up, and Roger cleared his throat behind him.

"Good news?" Roger asked.

"It looks like things may be going my way finally. I'll let you know tonight."

Clarissa had been standing on the side of the window that outlooked her front door. When Bain stepped out of his truck, she took a deep breath and stepped back from the door. She had been thinking about what he said at the vow writing event. She thought about what her problem was. It was true that Bain was and would always be an attractive man, but she had to pull herself together and give him the benefit of the doubt when it came to trusting him.

She couldn't imagine what it was like to be a model or to have people always wanting to take your picture. She could see how it was an invasion of privacy, and it was a wall she would have to get over if she wanted to be with Bain. Whether he modeled or not, he would still be in the paper and still be on someone's radar for gossip.

The doorbell broke her out of her reverie. She smoothed her blue dress over her hips and then put on a smile when she opened the door.

"Good morning," he said. "I came right over. Good, you're already dressed. Where did you want to go?"

She smiled. "Come in, I thought I'd cook."

When she closed the door behind him, he waited for her to lead him. She leaned in and gave him a quick kiss on the cheek.

Hopefully it would set the tone of them not being adversarial. She didn't wait to see his reaction. Instead, she took him by the hand and then led him into the kitchen. When they walked in, she heard him sigh in approval.

The table was set, and she had two warmers of food on the table.

"I thought you had to cook. To be honest, I'm starving," he said as he took a seat.

Clarissa smiled and sat down.

"I invited you over, so I started as soon as I got off the phone. I made pancakes, eggs, bacon, and homefries. I wasn't sure what you had a taste for." She watched him sit down and dig in. This was part of what she dreamed about. This was her and Bain being a normal couple. As long as they both were open and honest with each other, she would manage her insecurities.

"I know the day just started, but how are things in the media world?" she asked.

He looked up for a moment and then hesitated before smiling at her. "You know it's the same old thing. I was with Roger earlier today, and he's helping me manage a situation that has come up."

She smiled as he shared his day. She could see how she was being silly and foolish. "I'm sure whatever the issue is, you'll be able to fix it."

"It involves people, and that's what makes it so challenging," he said as he ate.

"You and Roger seem to work well together, so I think it'll be fine."

"Clarrie, I have to tell you something," Bain said as he put down his fork.

She smiled and covered his hand with hers.

"Bain, please, let me go first."

"Clarrie—"

She interrupted him.

"Bain, I'm sorry. I was being so silly. Here I am telling you I'm having an issue about trusting you, yet I'm breaking the rule by accusing you before you even do anything. I want us to have an open relationship where we can talk about anything. So I wanted to say you were right and I was wrong. I shouldn't accuse you or paint you guilty based on the past. Okay?"

Bain nodded his head slowly. Clarissa thought the declaration would make him happier, but now she was at a loss. A sense of trepidation and doom began to build within her.

"Bain, you had something you wanted to say?"

He looked at his food and then he looked back into Clarissa's eyes.

"I wanted to say that I had decided that I'm going to still model until I find another job."

"Okay, do you want another job?"

"I don't know."

"Hey, why don't we do this. I'm fine with you modeling. I know it will put you back in the limelight with all of the beautiful people, but it's okay. I'm feeling better now that we are talking about everything.

Bain choked. Clarissa got up and patted him on the back.

"Bain, are you okay?"

Bain nodded.

"Clarrie, I-I have a problem with Roger, and I'm not sure how to handle it."

Clarissa was all smiles now. He was asking her opinion, and they were trusting each other.

"I understand how it can be when you don't trust yourself to make the right decisions. But you're a smart person, and I think you should rely on your gut and do what you think is the best thing."

"My gut says full disclosure, but I'm sure that Roger would advise to just disseminate as little information as possible."

"Well, I can't get in between you and Roger, but I think you should follow your gut. I mean, at the end of the day, you've got to be able to look yourself in the mirror."

<h1 style="text-align:center">Fifteen</h1>

Clarissa had decided she was going to take the plunge. She knew what everyone had seen in the paper, and they would all think whatever they wanted to think. After breakfast with Bain yesterday, she knew they were in a good place. In two days' time, they would practice the processional walk for Hannah and Adam's wedding, and she wanted to make sure they were solid before that.

Clarissa thought a picnic would be the best way she could show Bain she was all in. She had called him over for lunch, and just like the last time, it took him no time at all to make it to her office. When he arrived, she pointed to the basket for him to carry, and they walked over to the public park that was three blocks away.

"I'm surprised you're keeping pace with me as we walk," Bain teased.

She smiled. "One of the things my aunt drilled into me is don't wear clothes that are so cute you can't function in an emergency. If I wear a dress, you can bet I can hitch it up to run. If you see me in shoes, you can also count on the fact that I know how to run and jump in those shoes, just in case."

"Why am I not surprised that these are the skills that you were taught from a woman whose name is Temperance," he laughed.

"I am most grateful for those teachings. There were a couple of dates where those teachings came in handy," she told him.

"Well, then, my thanks to her foresight."

"You are probably used to be with damsels in distress," she said as she laid out the food on the picnic table.

"Damsels in distress, huh?" he replied as he took out the drinks to help her.

"Yeah, you know, the ones that can't find their way to the car. Get lost in a two-block radius and need you to drive them everywhere for some unknown reason. They're the ones who send texts that just show they are distressed but give no relevant information, so you have to call them," she said, laughing.

"Okay, I know a lot of them, but I don't want to date them."

"Ah, you say it now, but when you are in model mode, you are larger than life and must save the little women."

He shook his head. "Is this your reason for thinking I may not always like you?"

"No, because I'm nothing like that and you stay. It's one of the many reasons I think you do like me. I'm definitely not your norm or easy."

"Yes, it was definitely your feisty nature and ability to stand against the wave that drew me to you."

Clarissa opened the pudding cup and began to eat.

"I'm sure that I detect some sarcasm in there, and I would correct you with the pudding, but I never waste pudding."

The sun was high, and they were sitting in the park, close to her job. A gentle breeze came every so often to cool them down. She could see there were people who came out and sat on the other benches. By dinner, it would be all over town that she and Bain were either on the mend or that there was indeed something going on.

She felt more relaxed. Now that they were being honest with one another, the tension was gone. This was the Bain she knew. He had to work in that model world, but her Bain always came back to her, and she and Bain were good.

A smile came to Clarissa's lips when she remembered what Daisy had said about Bain.

"He's got money, looks, and he only has eyes for you. What more could a woman ask for?"

If she was serious about building a life together with him, this was the way.

"Are you ready for the processional training?" she asked.

Bain rolled his eyes. "I mean, how bad can we mess up walking?"

"Don't ask that question. See what happened with us and the dress rehearsal?"

They ate and laughed some more until all the food was gone. Clarissa was about to write this off as a hit when it all came to a screeching halt.

"Clarissa Ann?"

Clarissa thought about not turning around. She thought if she didn't move, maybe her aunt would just go away, but breeding and manners won out. She turned to find Temperance standing at the end of the table.

Bain stood up to greet her. "Ms. Hastings," he said as he extended his hand. "We haven't formally met, so I wanted to introduce myself."

Temperance gave him a look. "You're right. We haven't officially met because you never gave Clarissa Ann a proper wedding with her family in attendance. So you'd like me to call you what?"

"Bain Parcel."

Thank goodness, her aunt shook his hand, and then her hawk-like gaze focused on her true prey.

"I thought we had discussed this situation."

Clarissa was saying *no, no, no* internally, but outside she looked at her aunt and said in even tones, "This isn't what you think."

"It isn't?" Temperance turned to Bain, who was sitting down on the bench. "It seems as though you have quite a hold on my niece."

"Since she has one on me, I'm okay with that."

"Too bad, I'm not."

"Family has a way of changing right in front of our eyes. It can be sudden when it happens, but it always happens."

Temperance gave him a long look and then she turned back to Clarissa.

"I can't believe I've raised you to be so reckless."

Clarissa wanted to interject, but she had to admit it was nice to see someone else deal with her aunt. No matter what she had said over the years, she was always the wrong one. She was always the one who had to capitulate.

"I think it's a bit harsh to call her reckless."

Temperance turned to face Bain. "Do you think you really have the right to intervene with the dealings that go on between my niece and me?"

"I'm Bain, and I want to be a part of her life."

"Like I said before, I know who you are. You've been in her life once before with disastrous results. I'm trying to understand what you're doing this time."

Temperance tuned back to Clarissa.

"I have never lied to you, Clarissa. There are a lot of things we disagree on, but I have always done what is best for you. Who is this man that he can talk to me about anything? After what we've talked about, how can you even talk to this man?"

Clarissa had an answer. Her aunt seemed like the embodiment of her not trusting Bain, and it made no sense. What could she say to her aunt, though? Bain was the man she loved but who had broken her trust, and now they are giving it another shot. While the truth may sound hopeful, it was not something she wanted to say to her aunt.

"Ms. Hastings, I'm the man your niece is in a relationship with," Bain said respectfully.

Temperance's eyebrow raised, and Clarissa saw her refocus her attention on Bain. "You seem to like relationships, Mr. Parcel."

"She's the only one for me."

Clarissa heard the words, and her faith was reaffirmed that she was on the right track.

Temperance took a step away from the table, looked between them, and then looked around the park.

"Ah, I get it now." It was the tone that had Clarissa on edge. It was the tone that said her aunt knew something that no one else knew. It was the tone of confidence that said no matter what the other person thought they had, she had a trump card.

Bain asked, "Just what do you get?"

"I understand this thing you are doing with you and Clarissa. It's just your indulgence while you are in town for publicity before you go back to your life with Natalya whatever her name is."

Clarissa took a quick peek around the park and saw there were other people who were idly standing by. She wasn't self-conscious before, but she was getting an inkling of oncoming doom. This was one of those moments when she wished she could just fall into the ground. But like so many other times, she would keep her head up and dare them to say something to her face.

"If you knew Natalya, you would know we are friends and co-workers. For you to think I would use Clarissa that way tells me you may be family, but you don't really know the woman you've raised. It's true, she's beautiful, but she's more than that. She's intelligent and a savvy business person. She's kind in ways others will never know, and she's humble. I'm sorry you don't appreciate and see those aspects of her."

Clarissa couldn't say a word. She heard Bain say the words, but surely those words were said just to quiet her aunt. If not, and those words were truly what Bain thought about her, she was twice the fool for not trusting him. He hadn't just said she was pretty, which would have been the most shallow thing to say; he had gone on about her as a person.

Temperance looked at the both of them; just when Clarissa was sure she was about to leave, and she was going to tell Bain how considerate he was to say those things, her aunt said her final words.

"I find those words to be very hollow. Maybe you forget this is a small town. There is only one hotel. Currently, I am staying in that hotel, and I had a very interesting conversation at breakfast with your co-worker Natalya, who has been here for the last couple of days, and she had a very different tale to tell."

Her aunt looked at him and then back to Clarissa.

"I told you, Clarissa Ann, to be careful. He's not like us, and he doesn't live by our same rules."

Bain interrupted her. "It's not like that—"

Temperance waved him off and continued to speak to Clarissa.

"When he is gone, you will still have to live here, and if you continue to indulge in this public foolishness, you will be the laughingstock again for this man."

With that, Temperance turned on her heel and left the two of them.

Clarissa remembered there was a saying that someone had said to her once—numb from the experience. She'd never understood that statement until just now. She wouldn't get up and go running; that would feed all of the gossipmongers. She wouldn't cry yet because she was still holding on to hope that Bain had an explanation.

"Is it true?" she whispered.

"Clarrie, it's not like she says."

Clarissa looked up to face Bain.

"Is Natalya here in Sweet Blooms?"

"Yes," he said quietly.

"Did she come to you when she arrived?"

"Yes, she did."

"Were you going to tell me?"

"I was, but I thought she would be gone and then it wouldn't matter. Things were going so well with us, and I didn't want to ruin it."

She started repacking the picnic basket.

"I think this lunch is over," she said.

Bain reached out and put his hands over hers.

"Clarrie—"

"Don't! Don't call me Clarrie. Don't say a word. I'm not going to run like some distressed damsel in distress. Let's pack up the basket, and you can take it back to the café. That's where I got it from. I'll be going back to my office."

"Let's talk."

Clarissa gave a cynical laugh. "The time to talk is over. I do want you to know that an omission is a form of lying as well. I hope you have a good day, Bain."

"What makes you think this will work?"

Roger stared at Natalya, standing by the trailer door. When he came in this afternoon, she had already removed some of Bain's pictures and put up hers.

"Listen, Roger, you already know I make money. I just found out they are going to take a couple of weeks. I can't be out that long."

Roger ran his hand through his hair. "I agree you can't be out that long, but that doesn't mean I need to represent you. Besides, you are forgetting a very important piece in this whole equation. You don't have any money to pay me."

Natalya waved that off.

"You mean I don't have any money to pay you now. You know I have money, and when they open my accounts, I can give it to you then. If you are as good as you seem to think you are, then you'll be making money off of me before they open up my funds again."

It's not a question of how good I am. I'm full. Everyone knows that I only take on three clients at a time. I offer quality service, and it pays all parties very well."

The door opened and in came an unhappy Bain. Roger focused on him.

"What happened?"

"She found out about Natalya."

"Ouch!"

"Me? Why does it matter? Is the press here already? I thought I got rid of them before I came."

Roger watched Bain hold his head as if that would make it alright.

"Tell me you were the one who told her at least?" Roger watched as Bain shook his head in denial.

"Her aunt Temperance told her," Bain said.

"Temperance? Ah, I met a woman in the hotel yesterday whose name was Temperance. We went out for breakfast and came back. You know we are in the only hotel this town has to offer, and she knows all the sites around here. I thought she was a very pleasant lady," Natalya finished with a firm nod.

Roger looked at Natalya and couldn't believe how bad his luck was.

"Natalya, how could you do this?"

Bain waved him off.

"It's not Natalya's fault. The fault is all mine because Clarissa was right. Omission is still a lie."

Natalya looked left to right. "I think someone needs to explain this to me."

"I'll explain over lunch. Bain?" Roger asked.

Bain waved them on and just put his head back and closed his eyes.

Sixteen

The expression was to strike while the iron was hot. That was the only reason her aunt wanted to have dinner tonight. After Bain and lunch, she went back to her office. She didn't take any calls or sign any documents; she just sat down and looked at the picture of her parents that she had in her drawer.

When she looked at them, they seemed so happy. She knew they had issues just like anyone else, but she couldn't imagine them having hers. She placed the picture back in her desk and prepared to go home and cook for her aunt. It was going to be a night of humble pie, but she had endured it once, and she could do it again.

It was seven, and Temperance was on time. Clarissa went to the door and didn't bother to smile, but she stepped in and greeted her aunt appropriately.

"Hello, Aunt."

"Clarissa Ann." Clarissa gritted her teeth. Tonight there would be no corrections. Her aunt had earned it today.

Clarissa could tell her aunt was feeling very triumphant. She had worn a green sundress. It did nothing to enhance the rest of her, but she was well accessorized with matching green drop earrings and very practical flat rubber bottom shoes. Clarissa was the one who hadn't bothered to dress up. When she came home, she changed into some jeans and a tee shirt.

Clarissa led her into the kitchen and sat her at the table.

"I remembered you don't like a lot of carbs, so I made meatloaf with rice as opposed to a pasta dish."

Temperance nodded. "Thank you for remembering."

Clarissa didn't really think there was anything to say, but still, they went through the motions. They ate dinner, and Temperance gave her customary response.

"Dinner was wonderful. It would have been better if you had been a little lighter on the pepper."

Temperance sat in the kitchen as Clarissa cleaned the dishes. When the silence was too much, Clarissa broke it.

"How much longer will you be staying in Sweet Blooms?"

"I'm thinking to leave in about four days. I think I should be good by then," she replied.

"Please let me know if you need any help or anything else," Clarissa offered.

"Clarissa, I know I'm not the most affectionate person, but I do what I do because I want you to be safe."

"I know that."

"Clarissa Ann, I've tried to raise you as best I could."

"I never doubted you were doing your best. I may not be the best person to show it, but I am grateful to you for raising me."

"Well, I guess we've danced around the elephant in

the room all night, so let me be the first one to acknowledge it. Why Bain again?"

Clarissa thought she had almost made it. She was at the numb point, but just hearing his name brought spikes of pain and feelings she wasn't sure she was ready to deal with.

"Bain and I have always been friends, and it was a short hop from there for us to develop feelings for one another."

"He's here for the wedding between Adam and Hannah if I read the article right."

"Yes, you know both Bain and I are in the wedding party, so we'll practice together since it's a big wedding."

"I want you to be careful around him."

"I already know he's a model and things are different," Clarissa said, doing her best to put aside what had already happened this afternoon. She knew her aunt would want to do a recap in one way or another; that was just her way.

"It's not that he has a different kind of job; the difference will always be that he is handsome, rich, and famous. Those are three characteristics he will never be able to get rid of."

"What does that mean exactly?"

"It means that she is supposed to be with other women and people who have those things. It's about like being with like. Really, what will the two of you have in common?"

Clarissa thought about them lying in the back of the truck and almost smiled.

"Aunt, I think people are together because of people and their personalities, not because of their tax bracket or their beauty."

Her aunt waved off the explanation. "I know you are a beautiful woman, but you need all three of those things to compete in his world."

"So you're saying without those three things I was never a serious consideration for Bain?"

Temperance nodded.

"You don't know men like him. He may be a nice person, but he's acting the way that his friends are."

"Well, after today I don't think we have to worry about those kinds of things."

"I just want you to know that this man isn't for you because you don't run in his circles.

"I'm curious, Auntie, what was the point of you telling me at the picnic instead of telling me while we were in my office?"

"I wanted to tell you when he was around. You know I'm not the kind of person to do something and then say I didn't do it. I wanted him to also have the chance to defend himself."

"I know you did what you thought was best, but the only thing I took away from this was you don't believe that I was ever going to be good enough for him. I think I would have preferred to learn that in the privacy of my own home without the park audience."

"I agree that it would have been less painful, but I think doing it this way was the only path open to me. You wouldn't listen when I told you he wasn't what he appeared. If I had told you that you weren't his type, then you would have scoffed and turned me away. This was the best way to get you to see him for what he truly was."

Clarissa realized the futility of the conversation and dropped it. When the dishes were done, she told her aunt she had to wake early.

Temperance looked around. "I guess that is the polite way of you telling me to leave."

Clarissa shook her head. "I'm not pushing you away. I just want to keep my commitments, especially after this afternoon."

Temperance nodded then pulled herself together. When she got to the door, she turned around and looked at Clarissa.

"Everything I do, I do for you, Clarissa."

"I know, but that doesn't mean it hurts less, Auntie."

With that, Temperance left to get into her car. Clarissa closed the door and leaned against it and then took a couple of deep breaths. Clarissa knew the cry was coming, but she wasn't ready yet. Thankfully for tonight, she was still numb.

Seventeen

Last night had been bad, but Clarissa was determined to make it through today's processional practice. She was trying to balance herself between not crying and not showing the way she really felt. She was feeling stupid and beaten. She had been here before, and she refused to let the rest of the world know she was so affected. Her pain was private, and it was hers and hers alone.

This would be the first time she would be seeing Bain, and she had been prepping since her dinner with her aunt. She had given herself several pep talks so she could face him. She'd explained to herself that it was only normal to try and give their relationship another go. There was no shame in trying.

She walked into the house and saw him standing in line. When he extended his arm, she paused. Lately, she was filled with moments of feast and famine. The feast was to just ignore his arm altogether, and the famine was to lean on him as if all was well. Instead, she found herself and took the middle option.

Annabelle came into view, and today she was back to her drill sergeant voice.

"Today, we will be walking to the dais that is set up outside. It's important that you have uniform steps and then know when to break off. So this is the way it will go. We will march out together, and then when you get to the second door, each couple will walk down the aisle and then turn and read their vows and separate."

Clarissa looked at the couples in front of her, and she wondered if she would be able to do this. They were the last couple, and it all seemed easy to get through until she realized how much of a perfectionist Annabelle was.

"Okay, Clarissa and Bain, it's your turn!"

They walked towards the door, her hand on his.

"Stop!"

Annabelle came charging like a bull.

"I need the two of you to walk in step as if you are marching. This will be recorded, and right now, you two aren't walking right."

Annabelle left and went to the side to watch again.

"You two can march whenever you're ready."

Both Clarissa and Bain spoke at the same time.

"Start with your left."

"Start with your right."

They started to walk, and on cue, Annabelle called out.

"Again!"

Clarissa looked to Bain. "What do you want to do, right or left start?"

"What's easier for you?"

"Really, Bain? Now you want to be accommodating? Make a decision and stick with it for once!"

"For once?"

Annabelle cleared her throat. "Any time!"

"Bain! On our right."

They took the first steps slowly at first, and then they made it to the door.

Annabelle clapped. "I'm happy you two remembered how to walk, but I'd like you to do so before the end of the wedding. Practice. Now the walk down the aisle and the vow."

Annabelle came over and handed them both the card. "You are supposed to read it in tandem."

Clarissa looked at the card and then looked at Bain. The card read, "Trust is the bridge that love rests on."

They walked down the path, and when they reached the dais, they turned and faced each other. Neither party said anything.

"Go on, Bain, I'd love to hear you say this. You should be used to saying things that may or may not be true."

"Clarissa—"

Annabelle called out to them. "Let's get it going!"

Bain looked at the card and then looked at Clarissa.

"Trust is the—"

Clarissa interrupted him. "Just stop," she whispered. "Let's at least leave as friends."

Bain let out a heavy sigh. "Clarrie…"

Clarissa turned towards Annabelle. "I'm sorry. I'm not feeling well. The walk will be no problem, and I'm sure Bain will be able to say the words without a problem."

She didn't look back, and she kept her head up as she walked out of the facility. It wouldn't be the first time she had left with everyone looking at her, and it probably wouldn't be last. She could hear her aunt's tone of disapproval. So much for not making a scene.

Natalya put her tea down on the table and looked at Roger.

"Why are you being mean to me today?" she asked. "I thought we were straight. I came here because I knew Bain wouldn't mind helping me and you are trying to make me into the bad person here."

Roger looked at Natalya and sighed. "You know it's not all your fault. It's true, you started it, but if I had told you I wasn't going to represent you and my ego hadn't gotten in the way, you would have left. Now Bain is paying for my greed and your blind desperation."

Natalya stood up and stamped her feet. She looked at the trailer and thought about how far she had fallen now that she was begging an agent to represent her and asking to be the tag along with her friend.

"I needed help. I don't know what I'm being accused of so I have no way to fight," Natalya said through clenched teeth. If she was going to be accused of something, she wanted to know exactly what it was.

"Friends don't eat friends."

Natalya flinched. "You can't say that to me! I would never do that to Bain."

Roger faced her and opened his hands. "It's not about what you thought you were doing; it's about what you did. You spoke to a woman named Temperance?"

Natalya nodded. "She was an older woman, alone, who needed a friend."

Roger laughed. "It's nice to know that guys aren't the only ones who get taken in by the bait. She is Clarissa's aunt."

Natalya rolled her eyes. "Clarissa is…"

Then her eyes popped open. "You can't mean *that* Clarissa!"

"Oh yes, and now she is beginning to see."

"Bain came back to Sweet Blooms to win her back and do a wedding for his best friend. All seemed like it was going well even though I think the start was bumpy."

Natalya folded her arms over her chest. "Well, this Clarissa isn't all she seems if she let my presence bother her. If Bain were mine, I'd fight for him and dare another woman to come by."

Roger stopped and gave Natalya a long look. "I'm not sure if I should be scared or not. Just to get this out of the way. You aren't harboring secret crush for him, are you?"

Natalya waved him off. "If I had wanted to have something with Bain, it would be done. Bain is my brother in a lot of ways, nothing more."

"Whew. Well, at least that's off the table."

Natalya clapped, and Roger gave her his attention. "We need to get back to the part of the conversation about Clarissa."

"Oh, yes! The issue isn't that you showed up. The problem is that you showed up and he didn't tell her."

"Ouch!"

"Yeah, that's what I said."

Natalya pointed to herself. "Why didn't he tell her about me?"

"He says he thought whatever it was you needed you'd be gone, so he didn't want to bring you up."

"And instead the woman brought it up and now he looks untrustworthy, hiding a friend who can't be trusted with the basics in life."

Roger looked at her, and she shrugged.

"I have been where she is, and it's not pleasant."

Roger nodded. "Well, they are not talking, and they have to do the wedding in a couple of days, and then they will separate. I think it's horrible, but on the other hand, I have to say he's told me to book him solid and that he doesn't want any time to rest at all."

Natalya sighed. "Well, this won't do. You must do whatever it is you need to do for him, and I'll do my part."

"Your part?" Roger asked skeptically.

Natalya shooed him away. "This is nothing for men to be concerned with. This is women's work."

Clarissa got an invitation from Hannah to meet in the café in town. She expected her to say that she was being excluded from the wedding party, and she braced herself to hear the news. It would hurt, but she'd keep her head up and move on.

Clarissa saw Hannah coming, and Hannah waved at her. She waited for her to sit and place her order before they talked.

"So Annabelle called me and wasn't sure if the two of you would be able to make it through the wedding. She thinks you two are the most attractive couple, but right now the whole town knows you two are at war."

Clarissa laughed. "At war, are we?"

Hannah leaned in. "At this point, we have to ask, are you on team ice queen or team hot bod? So far, I hear the numbers are neck and neck."

Clarissa smiled. "This town would find anything to bet on and make everything common gossip."

"We're friends, so you have to tell me if you're okay walking with Bain, or should I switch up the couples?"

Clarissa looked at Hannah and had to look away so she wouldn't see her eyes watering.

"Hey girlfriend, what's going on?"

Clarissa looked up. "I thought you were coming to tell me I was out of the wedding."

Hannah sat back. "Ah, I can see how that would be a different conversation. Clarissa, no matter how it started, you do know we're friends, right?"

Clarissa looked up through her watery gaze and nodded. "I do now."

"So is Bain in or is he out?"

"He's the best man, so I think he needs to stay in."

The waitress brought her coffee, and Hannah took a sip before continuing.

"Well, that means whatever it is, the both of you need to try to keep it together. This wedding is going to be televised if I understand all the media hoo hoo going on around me."

"Great, everyone will see the woman Bain left."

Eighteen

"I think you should listen before you do anything." Those were the words Hannah had said to her on the phone ten minutes ago. When Clarissa had asked for some clarity, she wouldn't give it. Instead, she said, "Just remember what I said."

A few moments later, she heard a commotion outside, and Jessica said, "No, you don't have an appointment." Seconds later, the door was pushed open and Natalya walked into her office.

Jessica was red in the face as she tried to explain. "Clarissa, I'm so sorry. I tried to explain to her that she needed an appointment."

Natalya turned on Jessica and said in short, biting tones, "And I tried to tell her that what I need to discuss needs no appointment."

Clarissa watched Natalya waltz into the room and take a seat in the chair. Natalya was everything Clarissa feared she would be. She appeared in charge, perfectly groomed, and she was wearing blue jeans and a shirt. She was the type of woman who woke up beautiful and then put on makeup, so the rest of the world would think they had a chance.

"Call off your watchgirl."

Clarissa looked at Jessica. "It's okay. I'll take care of it."

Jessica gave Natalya a look and then walked out of the room.

"How can I help you?" Clarissa said in an even voice.

Natalya looked at Clarissa and then nodded.

"I can see why he loves you."

"I don't know what you thought you were going to accomplish by coming in here today."

"I thought I would help a friend out."

Clarissa cleared her throat. "The definition of friend has certainly changed."

Natalya put her hand up. "Let me stop you before you say the wrong thing. Bain and I have never been romantically involved."

"It's fine, and I really don't care, Natalya. Did Bain send you here?"

"No, I need you to understand some things."

Clarissa interrupted her. "Really, I don't need to know anything. What happens between you and Bain is your business. I don't really care or want to know."

Natalya stood up and paced in front of Clarissa's desk. "You are just as stubborn as Bain."

Clarissa stood up and then walked towards her office door. "I want to thank you for coming by, but you wasted your time. There is no Bain and me."

"Do you know he told me you are the only woman he has ever met that he's thought about having children with?"

Clarissa had grabbed the doorknob of her office door, but she stopped suddenly.

"Natalya, I think you should—"

Natalya interrupted. "He said he loved you because you loved him for himself and he wasn't sure there was anything there except a jock and a pretty face. You saw the man beneath, and he wanted to be a better person because of it."

Clarissa leaned her forehead against the door and then took a deep breath. "Natalya, I appreciate what you are saying, but the problem between Bain and I is trust."

"You are blaming him for being stupid. Certainly, you know he is a man. He will make many decisions that will make no sense, and only in hindsight will he be able to see the error of his ways. For each time he makes a mistake, will you throw him away?"

Clarissa turned around and faced Natalya.

"What do you want, and why are you here?"

"I told you. I am here for a friend. Will you listen to me first? Then, if you still want me to leave, I will."

Clarissa looked at Natalya and nodded. The sooner she listened, the sooner she'd leave. "Fine."

"You have no reason to believe me, but this is the truth. Bain is helping me because I called in a favor that he couldn't say no to."

Clarissa watched and waited. Could this woman say anything that would change things?

"Go on, I'm listening."

"When Bain lost his football career, he came to me with Roger. Roger told me to take a chance and bring Bain onto a shoot. He knew nothing. If only you could have seen Bain then. He was tripping over cameras and just making a fool of himself. I was sure that this was the worst favor I had ever granted. The shoot was a romantic getaway ad. He was photogenic. His coloring matched mine perfectly in front of the camera, and our bodies were proportionally idealistic."

Clarissa sat down across from Natalya. "It sounds so cold when you say it."

Natalya shrugged. "In this business, it is very cold. You either have the look, or you don't. People want to see you in their ads, or they don't. No one has time to coddle anyone, and things move fast.

"At any rate, I gave Bain a chance, and when we were in front of the camera, they said he would be a star if he could smile. I asked him to smile, and he said he was, but the cameraman said he looked sad.

"I pulled him to the side, and I told him this may be the only chance he had to make a lot of quick money. The cameraman called us back in. He told us to pose. He asked us to give him romance and love.

"Bain held me in his arms and looked into my eyes. He said, 'I'm doing this for us, Clarrie.' The cameraman never heard him. Throughout the shoot, when we would have to hold poses, he would say random phrases like 'I love you, Clarrie.' 'You are the light, Clarrie.'

"Needless to say, he was a hit. And it really is all history from there. He built a reputation being this man in perpetual love because he was and still is. You are that woman. Don't let the fact that I called a favor in because my career was having some difficulty destroy the boy and the dream."

Clarissa listened to her, and the words sunk into her soul. What could she do? She would have to accept that Bain just made a bad call in not telling her about Natalya. Even if she did that, how would she fix things with Bain?

Natalya interrupted her thoughts. "Stop, girl, the thinking is going so fast and furious that it's giving me a migraine."

Clarissa sat back on her couch and sighed. "Oh, I don't think it matters. Our argument has escalated to two teams in the town. I don't think I can fix this with him. I still think that he was wrong and he should have told me about you, but you're right. I could forgive him and move on. If I knew he was willing to do the same.

"It doesn't matter, Natalya; the core problem is still there. It's about trust."

Natalya got up and smiled at Clarissa.

"I'll tell you what I would do, and then you can decide. If I thought he was my one true love, I'd throw myself at his feet and start over."

Clarissa knew she had to clean up her past before she could enjoy her future. That was the only reason she was at the hotel to see her aunt. She realized that by not talking to her aunt, she had put herself in a cage. That cage was constantly opening and closing on her happiness with Bain.

Clarissa had listened to Natalya. They weren't friends, but they could talk to each other because they cared about what happened to Bain. If she was going to be able to overcome her problems and be what Bain needed, she needed to start with her own confidence, and this was where it had all started.

Her aunt was sitting primly at a table in the room, watching her.

"Aunt Temperance, I came to tell you first that I'm going to invite Bain over, and hopefully he will take me back. I'm going to try to live the happily ever after." Clarissa had practiced saying this so many times last night, and every time it came out different. Now she had said it and given it life in front of her aunt, and it was done. There was a sense of relief that she had said it, and there was an equal sense of trepidation. She still had to face Bain, and she had to get through her aunt's reaction.

Temperance sighed and then gestured for Clarissa to sit at the small round table with her.

"It's not my intention to make your life miserable," her aunt began.

Clarissa didn't relax hearing that phrase. She had been caught one too many times with her aunt's one-two comments. The first one made sense and made you relax, and the second one could rip your heart out.

"I wanted to make sure you led a long life and didn't let impulsiveness take you down a bad path." Her aunt straightened her back. "Your mother was vibrant, amazing, and so lively. She always had been, but she was also impulsive. An ounce of prevention could have saved them both."

Clarissa didn't know what to say. She had heard the stories about her parents. They were in love. They were bold, and now she had to admit that no one had ever talked about how often she was with other family members or nannies until they came back. The words were hard to get out, but Clarissa had already come this far; now she'd go all the way.

"I thought you didn't like my mother," she whispered.

Her aunt sighed. "I can't tell you that I liked her at all. What I can say is that I loved my sister, and there was nothing I wouldn't do for her. The problem was never me doing things for her. The problem I always had was that everyone expected me to do things for her, and whatever it was that I was doing was never as important."

Clarissa was confused, and it must have shown.

"When your parents died, I was going to leave and become a chef with a man that I fancied myself in love with. In retrospect, I don't suppose it was anything but a flare of two people who had a passion for cooking."

Clarissa put her hand to her chest. "I never knew."

"A lot of people never knew, and they didn't care."

Clarissa remembered she had once found a box in the attic of the old house filled with cooking tools and books. When she'd asked her aunt about it, she had said the box was a part of lost dreams. She had assumed those lost dreams were her parents'.

"I'm sorry, Auntie. Sorry that you had to give up so much."

Temperance reached her hand out and placed it over Clarissa's.

"I want you to understand this, and we'll never have to talk about it again. I don't regret taking you in, Clarissa Ann. When my sister passed, you were all there was that was left of her. You look like her. You have mannerisms like her. In some ways, I found my sister again when I got you as a child. I don't regret a single day of having you then or now."

Clarissa heard the words, and her eyes started to tear up. She heard the sincerity in her aunt's voice, and she understood some of the past a little better than she did before.

"Thank you."

"I'm glad we were able to have this talk. Now that that's behind us, we can address the other issue. Bain."

Clarissa looked at her aunt, and she gave a short laugh. Her aunt would always be the way she was. She was the backbone of morality, and she believed in maintaining the reputation and good name of a woman. She may dress different and move through the times, but she would always be who she is.

"I love you, and that's why I'm asking."

"It's not Bain that's the problem. I'm the one who feels insecure."

"He didn't tell you about the model," her aunt countered.

"It's true, but I should have talked to him. Instead, I was waiting for something to break us up or for him to do something that was going to show me that I wasn't enough for him. When the thing with Natalya came up, I didn't even give him a fair shot to explain what was wrong."

Her aunt sat back and sighed.

"I can see you've thought about this a lot."

Clarissa nodded. "I have. I love Bain. I need to trust in that love and give it a chance to flourish."

"Since your mind is set, then the only thing I can say is good luck."

Clarissa looked up, surprised.

"Don't look like I've become some weird person all of a sudden. You are braver than I would be, so I have to acknowledge that. If you are willing to risk it all to be with him, I hope that all goes well. No matter what I do, I do it because I love you. That probably doesn't make it easier for you, but it makes it so I can sleep at night knowing I did the best thing by you."

Clarissa got up and hugged her aunt.

"I love you, Auntie."

"I love you too, Clarissa Ann."

Clarissa closed her eyes. "That name," she moaned.

Her aunt's embrace tightened. "Don't push your luck. You've got the okay for Bain; we'll compromise on the name.

Clarissa laughed. "Of course, Auntie."

Nineteen

Clarissa had invited Bain over to her house. After talking with her aunt, she had felt empowered and ready to face anything. Now that the morning had arrived, she was wondering where all that bravado had come from.

She hadn't seen Bain since the last rehearsal. The wedding was in two days. She knew she had to face up to her shortcomings and make this right. This probably wasn't the best way to do this. She thought back to all of the things they'd done since he'd been back in Sweet Blooms. All of the shenanigans he'd had to endure had been to make her feel secure and to trust him. It was funny how hindsight was, and it was never flattering. Today there wouldn't be any agreements or deals; it would just be them.

She had put on a blue flowing sundress and pulled out some blue ballerina flats. She'd been up for the last three hours, fixing the house, choosing her outfit, and just plain fidgeting. When the doorbell rang, she practically jumped out of her skin. She took a deep breath and then smoothed the material of her dress.

She wondered if she should wait so he wouldn't think she was waiting for him. She hesitated, and then he knocked.

"I'm coming."

She pulled open the door, and there he was standing in front of her. She couldn't move. All of that practicing, and it went right out the window when she saw him. He was more today. He had on blue jeans and a maroon tee shirt.

He looked fit and relaxed. Somehow he was waiting at the door, but the way he leaned against the door frame made it look like he was always posing for a commercial.

"Are you ready to talk?"

"Excuse me?" She expected a lot of words from him this morning; those words hadn't been one of her options.

"I'm just saying we have been going through the wringer because you won't go all in. I'll work with you, Clarrie, but we're dead in the water if you won't talk to me."

Clarissa nodded. "It's true I didn't recognize what the problem was so I couldn't resolve it, and I couldn't ask you for help because it was a me problem."

Bain stepped into her house and closed the door behind him. He put his hand under her chin and then leaned down and placed a kiss on her lips. She hadn't expected him to be this understanding. She had prepared herself to grovel, but instead Bain came to the door knowing the problem and with open arms.

"I knew what the problem was. I knew you didn't feel worthy. I have already taken out a banner ad in town with your picture."

Clarissa pulled back. "What?"

Bain shrugged. "I was getting desperate; the wedding was getting closer. I was concerned that you may not find the answer beforehand."

"What's on the banner?"

"The truth. It says, 'This is a picture of Bain Parcel's most valuable treasure.'"

Clarissa had to hold back the tears that threatened to fall. Clarissa laughed and laid her head against his shoulder. "That is so nice of you to say."

Bain rubbed her back and held her in his embrace.

"I'm not really all that nice, Clarrie. You make me a better person. You're strong in the face of adversity. I know you have a sense of loyalty that is rare. You're attractive, but most importantly, you are smart and compassionate. Holding you in my arms makes me remember when we were married and helps me to see how well we'll be in the future."

She heard his words, and they fell into her soul and flourished. This is what she was looking for; this is what she knew she deserved. If they were going to have problems, they'd face them together. She wouldn't be alone anymore. She knew she deserved more.

"Are you ready to start on our forever life, Clarrie?"

She pulled back and looked him in the eye. "Yes, I'm finally ready."

I hope you've enjoyed Evan and Cassandra's story. Check out Book five in the Love Happens Series *Sweet Inspirations* and read Henry and Elizabeth's story.

Sign up to my newsletter to receive updates on new releases, sale promotions, and free books.

susanwarnerauthor.com

www.ingramcontent.com/pod-product-compliance
Lightning Source LLC
Chambersburg PA
CBHW071829190726
48292CB00005B/1678